Slowly, Zack [barcode: W9-DHR-505]
His Mouth from Temple's Lips

and pressed swift kisses along the column of her throat. Cool caution began to fight the hot passion within her and she stirred and pushed gently, almost regretfully, at his shoulders.

Reluctantly, he moved away, but his eyes still held her in their grasp. "It is inevitable, little wildcat. Can't you see?" His voice was a caress. "You will be mine. I knew it when I first saw you."

Temple struggled for control. She tore her gaze away from his. "I—I think we should go now. I want to go home. . . ."

ELAINE CAMP
has known since the age of ten that she wanted to be a writer. Now she is both a reporter and an accomplished novelist. Her journalist's training comes in handy when she travels, helping her to notice the details that later turn up in her books. *To Have, To Hold* is her first Silhouette Romance.

Dear Reader:

At Silhouette we try to publish books with you, our reader, in mind, and we're always trying to think of something new. We're very pleased to announce the creation of Silhouette First Love, a new line of contemporary romances written by the very finest young adult writers especially for our twelve-to-sixteen-year-old readers. First Love has many of the same elements you've enjoyed in Silhouette Romances—love stories, happy endings and the same attention to detail and description—but features heroines and situations with which our younger readers can more easily identify.

First Love from Silhouette will be available in bookstores this October. We will introduce First Love with six books, and each month thereafter we'll bring you two new First Love romances.

We welcome any suggestions or comments, and I invite you to write to us at the address below.

Karen Solem
Editor-in-Chief
Silhouette Books
P.O. Box 769
New York, N.Y. 10019

ELAINE CAMP
To Have, To Hold

Silhouette *Romance*

Published by Silhouette Books New York

America's Publisher of Contemporary Romance

SILHOUETTE BOOKS, a Simon & Schuster Division of
GULF & WESTERN CORPORATION
1230 Avenue of the Americas, New York, N.Y. 10020

Copyright © 1981 by Deborah Camp

Distributed by Pocket Books

ISBN: 0-671-57099-4

First Silhouette printing August, 1981

10 9 8 7 6 5 4 3 2 1

Map by Tony Ferrara

America's Publisher of Contemporary Romance

Printed in the U.S.A.

To my parents,
who never laughed at my dreams

To Have,
To Hold

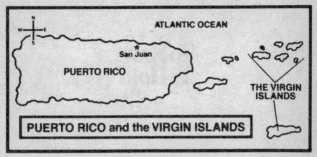

ATLANTIC OCEAN

San Juan

PUERTO RICO

THE VIRGIN ISLANDS

PUERTO RICO and the VIRGIN ISLANDS

JOST VAN DYKE ISLAND

HANS LOLLIK ISLAND

Magens Bay

British
United States

TORTOLA ISLAND

ST. THOMAS

Charlotte Amalie

ST. JOHN

NORMAN ISLAND

CARIBBEAN SEA

ST. CROIX

VIRGIN ISLANDS

Chapter One

The majestic cruise ship eased out of the harbor and headed for the open sea. Black smoke drifted from the brightly colored stack, and the throaty sound of the horn drifted to Temple Anderson's ears.

Temple blinked rapidly, her lashes wet with tears. With an exasperated sigh she swiped at them and tried to still her trembling lower lip. She watched the white ship recede until it was no more than a dot on the horizon.

It's like watching my dream vanish, she thought. That ship is taking all my hopes and all my ambitions.

She felt the bitterness settle in her heart and she turned and looked around her for the first time. The harbor was bustling with activity. Stacks of crated fruits and vegetables surrounded her. Loud voices sounded all around her and she watched the men to whom they belonged scurry along the decks of bobbing boats and the slippery wharves. Fishermen, she thought, as she surveyed their lean bodies and the massive nets they were folding.

Her gaze moved past the harbor to take in the green hills of St. Thomas. Here and there a red-tiled roof peeked from beneath the dense foliage, and large, brightly flowered bushes provided splashes of startling color.

Temple picked up her suitcase, walked back to the street that skirted the harbor and signaled for a taxi, which braked to a stop beside her. The cabby flashed her a gleaming white smile.

"Where to, lady?"

"Where to?" Temple blinked at his dark face for a moment, then shrugged. "Take me to the Mountain Top Hotel, please."

The cabby nodded and stuck a tape in the dashboard cassette player as he pulled back into traffic. A country-western song blared from the speaker behind her, and Temple smiled, finding it odd to hear such music in this tropical spot. The cabby began singing harmony with the recorded singer, glancing from time to time in the rearview mirror to catch Temple's reactions.

Temple frowned and kept her eyes glued to the side window. I'm glad somebody's happy, she thought, but my life is ruined, so why should I pretend to care?

Her ears began popping as the cab climbed the steep hill to the Mountain Top Hotel. She swallowed, trying to relieve the sharp pain in her inner ear.

"You a tourist, lady?"

Temple nodded and swallowed again.

"You stay long?"

"I hope not—but it looks like I might."

"You don't like it here?"

10

"I like it," Temple replied with a shrug. "I just don't want to stay here, that's all. I want to go home."

"Where's that? America?"

"No, Puerto Rico—San Juan."

"You don't sound like you're from San Juan."

"I wasn't born there. I've lived there for three years, though."

The cabby turned into the parking lot of the hotel, then twisted to face Temple. "It's not far to San Juan."

"I know." Temple opened her purse and searched for her wallet. "But it's far enough when you can't afford a ticket. How much do I owe you?"

"You don't have money to go home?"

Temple tried to keep the disappointment from her voice. "That's right. Now, how much do I owe you?"

"Fifty cents."

Temple gave him a startled look. "Fifty cents?" She blushed when she saw the twinkle in his eye. "No, really. How much?"

The cabby's face wrinkled in a smile. "Fifty cents, lady. You let me sing, so you get a discount." He held out his tan palm.

Temple felt her bottom lip tremble again as she placed the coins in the man's hand. "Thank you. You're very kind."

The cabby waved and gave her a wink as she stepped from the vehicle. She watched the dark blue car disappear down the hill, thinking that there went the nicest person she'd met all day.

She sighed and walked into the hotel. It's not

as crowded as it was this morning, she thought as she made her way to the sunken bar that provided a breathtaking view of the Caribbean. She sat down, the suitcase on the floor beside her chair, and waited for the bartender to spot her.

A few minutes later the young man turned from a customer and his eyes widened. "Temple! You back again?" He glanced at his wristwatch and frowned. "But—it's—"

Temple raised her hands to stop his words. "I know. It's after two o'clock. The ship has sailed."

The bartender shook his head and tossed some fresh bananas into a blender already full of other ingredients. "I guess . . . I mean . . ."

Temple nodded. "I didn't get the job."

The blender whirred for a few seconds, then was silent. The bartender poured a measure of the banana daiquiri into a glass and handed it to Temple.

"This one's on the house, Temple. Sorry about the job. What happened?"

Temple sipped the drink and shrugged. "Bad timing—as usual. I don't want to talk about it, Scrappy."

"You going back home?"

"How?" Temple asked, spreading her hands in a helpless gesture. "I spent all my money getting here. I haven't enough left to get back."

"Borrow it, from a finance company, maybe."

"Scrappy, you have to have credit to borrow, and I don't. Besides, all I need is *another* bill!"

Scrappy tapped a finger against his temple

and winked. "Let me think about this. I'll come up with a solution for you, don't you worry."

Temple watched as he moved around the oval bar and served the other customers. Funny, she thought, how I feel as if I've known Scrappy for a long time. Yet we only met two days ago. She paused in her introspection. Two days? It was already beginning to feel like forever. I wonder what Scrappy's last name is, she thought. She listened to him talk to the other customers and wondered if his accent had roots in England or Australia.

She examined the other people gathered around the bar. An elderly couple was talking to Scrappy about their visit to St. John, a nearby island. A few chairs down from them three girls were chattering about the tour they had just taken of St. Thomas. Each girl had a camera, and they were busy snapping pictures of Scrappy and the bar, no doubt to show off to their friends back home.

I wish I could enjoy the scenery, Temple thought. St. Thomas is a lovely island, but somehow I just don't feel like soaking up the atmosphere.

She looked past the bar windows to the glistening sea. Sunbeams danced across its choppy surface, and Temple thought she'd never seen an ocean quite so lovely. What color is it? she wondered. Turquoise? Aqua? She shifted her gaze to the towering coconut palms that framed her view of the sea. A few additional tourists were standing underneath them, on the terrace surrounding the bar.

It really is lovely here, she thought. I wish I could forget my troubles and just go sightseeing, or lie on the white sand beaches getting tanned. She knew the water would be deliciously warm, just as it was off the coast of San Juan, and perfect for swimming.

Suddenly she felt an almost irresistible urge to race out of the hotel and into the sea. It almost seemed that her troubles would wash away in that magic water. No, she told herself. Don't be silly. Trouble is here to stay.

Temple ran her hand through her short black hair and stared into her drink. She thought of the small apartment she had lived in back in San Juan and longed to be there now.

No, she reminded herself. It wasn't hers anymore. She'd been so sure she would get this job that she had sold everything and given up the lease on her apartment.

She clenched her hands at the thought. What a crazy, impulsive action that had been. Her parents had been right. She kept reaching for rainbows instead of keeping her feet planted firmly on the ground.

Her thoughts drifted to Jeremy, and she wondered if she should have married him.

What would that have solved? she mused. I'd just have different problems. I'd be dying of boredom. Jeremy is so conventional, so predictable. Being married to an accountant just isn't my cup of tea.

She recalled his last letter. He had taken a job with a firm in New York; there were more opportunities there than in San Juan. He'd followed her while she lived out her foolish fantasy, he said, and now it was her turn to be sensible and follow him. He wanted her to come home to New York. Her parents wanted her to come home.

She swirled the pale yellow liquid in her glass and smiled sadly. I don't *want* to go home! she thought. New York's not my home anymore; I live *here*—in the Caribbean!

She remembered how she had felt suffocated in New York. Her parents meant well, she thought, but they were so protective! She could almost hear them now, trying to talk her out of leaving the States. Her mother had cried, and her dad had all but begged her to marry Jeremy, not to take the chance that she might lose him if he decided not to follow her.

"Play it safe," he had said. "Jeremy's a fine young man, and you're just too young to know what love really is. Stay here in New York; let Jeremy have his career, and you can start having a family."

Temple's blood boiled at the recollection. What's the big hurry in marrying, anyway? she asked herself. I'm only twenty-four and hardly an old maid!

Still, she admitted, their pleas continued to haunt her even after three years of being on her own. Sometimes, when she felt really down, she wished she were back at her parents' house. Life was simple there. There were no money problems. No doubts.

"And I felt dead there." She surprised herself when she spoke the words aloud. I just existed.

Just went through the motions of living, she added silently.

She finished the last of her drink and felt the anger and hurt slice through her. If only that job singing on the cruise ship had materialized. What awful luck she had.

Fingering the empty glass, she wondered if she should try to find a waitress job. The idea made her stomach lurch. Not another waitress job, she thought with a moan. I want to write home and tell Mom and Dad and Jeremy that I've got a *real* job. I want to prove to them that I can make it!

They knew she was living hand to mouth now. They kept dropping hints about the "good life" she could live in the States. What had that last item been about Jill? She recalled the passage: "Your sister and the kids went to the museum yesterday. Tonight they're going to a play. There are so many things to do in New York. Don't you miss them?"

She shrugged her shoulders. Sure, she missed them. But not enough to go back to a life that had stifled her and give up on her dreams of independence and a singing career.

A hand curled around her empty glass where it sat on the table. Temple jumped and looked up to see Scrappy's smiling face.

"Sorry I took so long to get back to you."

"I understand. I just came at a busy time."

"It's *always* busy here, Temple."

Temple bit her lip, then forced herself to ask the question. "Do you think they'd hire an extra waitress?"

"Now wait a minute, songbird!" Scrappy took her glass and refilled it. "I might have an idea. Don't go jumping at a waitress job, not yet."

Temple sat up straighter in her chair. "You know of a place that might hire a singer?"

"Not off hand, but I do know someone who might know of a place."

"Who?" Temple felt the energy flow through her.

"A customer." Scrappy glanced at his watch. "He should be here in a few minutes; he usually comes in at about this time. He has a lot of connections."

Temple squirmed in her chair. "I hope he can help me." She smiled at Scrappy. "I really don't want to wait tables again."

"I don't blame you, songbird." Scrappy's eyes moved to focus on a spot beyond her shoulder. His brows rose and he nodded. "Here he is now."

Temple turned in her chair, and her heart skipped a beat when she saw the man striding toward them, a lazy smile on his lips.

He had a commanding aura about him, an aura of wealth and power. Dressed in a dark suit, white shirt, and gray tie, he stood out among the bright tropical colors of the bar and the casually dressed patrons.

Thick, dark brown hair topped a wide forehead, and his dark brows only served to emphasize almost black eyes that actually seemed to glitter. His nose was straight, his cheekbones high and well formed, and his mouth wide and generous.

Temple caught her breath at the sight of him

17

and had to stop herself from pressing her hand to her throat. She felt drawn to him. She blushed and wondered how just the sight of this man could affect her so strongly.

"Good afternoon, Scrappy."

His voice was soft, yet deep and totally masculine. His eyes touched Temple, and she shivered. The brief contact left her breathless, even frightened, and she averted her gaze from him and tried to gather her wits.

"Afternoon, Zack. Got a fresh container of banana daiquiris here."

"Good, good." He eased his tall frame into one of the seats and folded his lean hands. "It seems there are more tourists every year."

"Yeah, it sure does." Scrappy turned in Temple's direction and cleared his throat. "Zack, this is Temple Anderson. She's in a bit of a bind, and I thought you might be able to help."

"Oh?" The man raised an eyebrow. "In what way?"

Temple cringed and wished Scrappy would just drop the subject. She didn't know why, but for some reason she didn't want to seem helpless in front of this man.

"Well, she came here from San Juan because she heard there was an opening for a singer on one of the cruise ships, but she didn't get the job. Do you know of anyplace on the island that might need a singer?"

Temple sighed and collected her courage. She lifted her lashes and looked directly at the man.

"Which cruise line rejected you?"

Temple swallowed, too aware of the pulse that beat nervously in her throat. "The Saint Lines."

Scrappy set the pitcher of drinks down with a bang and stared at Temple. "The Saint Cruise Lines?"

Temple stared back at him. "Yes. Why?"

Scrappy shook his head. "Temple . . ."

The other man glanced warningly in his direction, and Scrappy fell silent.

"Did you audition, Miss Anderson?"

Temple tore her eyes from Scrappy. "No. You see, I got a tip that *The Calypso* had lost a singer, so I sold everything I had to afford passage here. I know it sounds stupid, but I was just so sure . . ." Her voice trailed into silence. "Anyway, when I went to the ship, the cruise director said I didn't have enough experience. He wouldn't even listen to me!" The memory sent a new wave of anger surging through her, and she squared her shoulders and lifted her chin. "He said the owner of the line *insisted* on experienced talent. He absolutely refused to grant me an audition. He told me that he could tell I wasn't of the caliber the owner required."

The man sipped his drink, then asked in a quiet voice, "I take it you feel the owner of the cruise lines is unjust."

"Absolutely!" Temple warmed to her topic. "I should think he'd *want* to discover new talent, instead of turning it away."

"Temple . . ." Scrappy's voice was a warning.

Temple glanced at him, then turned back to the man named Zack. "I think the owner is being completely unfair. The *least* he could do is audition new talent."

Scrappy moaned and shook his head, and Temple stared at him in confusion.

"Miss Anderson," the man said to her slowly, as if he were selecting each word carefully, "you may possibly be correct. In that case, do you think I should give you another chance?"

Temple looked at him for a moment, trying to follow his train of thought. What did he mean, "*another* chance"?

He sipped his drink again and then leaned toward her, his elbow almost touching hers. "I am the owner of the Saint Cruise Lines, Miss Anderson. I am Zachary St. James."

His words hit Temple like a blow, and she jerked away from him. She saw his dark eyes glitter, and then his mouth twitched as if he were smothering a grin.

"You . . . you!"

He nodded. "Yes. Me."

Humiliation filled her, then anger. "You should have told me right away! You let me make a fool of myself! You had no right!"

"Perhaps." He leaned back in his chair. "But I doubt if you would have been honest if you'd known."

He smiled, and Temple thought how startlingly white his teeth looked against his tan. He raised his glass in a toast and finished the drink, then shook his head at Scrappy's offer of another.

"I repeat, should I give you another chance?"

"Another chance? You've never even given me a *first* chance!"

He smiled again. "Well, I might be able to help you secure a position here on the island. I know the owner of the Yellowbird Club. She already has a piano player, but she might hire a singer, too."

Temple looked at Scrappy and caught his quick grin. She tried to still the surge of hope and excitement she felt, warning herself to watch out for further pipe dreams. "I'd . . . appreciate any help you could offer, Mr. St. James. I've heard of the Yellowbird Club. It's supposed to be one of the best nightspots on the island, isn't it?"

"Yes, that's right." He stood and removed two bills from his pocket. He placed them on the bar and nodded at Scrappy. "Delicious, as usual, Scrappy. See you tomorrow." He turned to Temple. "Shall we go meet the owner?"

"Now?" Temple felt her nerves stretch and quiver.

"Yes. Why procrastinate?"

"I'm . . . I'm . . ." Temple searched for an excuse, and her gaze fell on her small suitcase, which now contained all her worldly goods. "I can't; I just can't walk in there with everything I own and ask for a job."

He looked coldly at her. "If you really want this job, Miss Anderson, I suggest we go now, suitcase or no." He glanced at his watch. "The owner will have time to hear you now; you may not be so lucky later."

He strode from the bar. Temple watched him go, then turned to Scrappy with pleading eyes. Scrappy shrugged; there was plainly nothing more he could do to help her. Temple's gaze found the three girls with the cameras. They were watching the man, and Temple noticed their flushed cheeks and longing expressions. She looked around for Zachary St. James and saw him standing by the entrance, an impatient frown on his lips.

Quickly, suddenly afraid she might lose this chance, she grabbed her things and joined him. He led her outside to a chocolate-brown sports car, and Temple smiled to herself. How appropriate, she thought. His car matches him perfectly—long and sleek and probably very fast.

She ran her hands over the soft leather seats and breathed in the musky odor of hide. The carpet beneath her sandaled feet was thick and plush. If she hadn't known when he walked in that this was a man used to money and power, this car would have told her so.

"Tell me, was my cruise director rude to you?"

Temple started to tell him that the director had been an ogre, but she hesitated and tried to recall his exact attitude. She sighed.

"Not really rude," she answered. "It's just that I wanted that job so much, and he wouldn't even listen to me." She looked down at her clasped hands and forbade the tears that threatened to fill her eyes. "He . . . he wasn't rude, though. Not really."

He was silent, and Temple turned her gaze in

his direction. His eyes met hers and she looked away.

"Maybe you'll have better luck at the Yellowbird."

"I hope so. I do appreciate this."

"I know. You've told me." He shrugged. "All I'm going to do is introduce you to a friend of mine." His dark eyes flicked over her. "The rest is up to you."

Temple reached into her purse and pulled out her compact. Flipping it open, she examined herself in the small mirror. Large blue eyes framed by sooty lashes stared at her as she patted her hair into place. With her fingers she arranged her spiky bangs and smoothed the hair at the back of her neck into place. Then she applied a touch of powder to her nose and shut the compact with a snap.

A sixth sense told her that another pair of eyes was focused on her and she glanced to the side in time to see Zachary St. James's intent gaze before he once more turned his attention to the street before him.

I wonder if he likes what he sees? Temple mused as she replaced the compact in her purse. She knew she wasn't classically beautiful, but she also knew she was attractive to men. She glanced at her small breasts and narrow hips and wished she had voluptuous curves. That's probably what he goes for, she decided. Full-figured women with sultry, sexy looks.

She felt the car slow and pulled several folded sheets of paper from her purse. "I have a few songs here. I hope they're the type of thing your friend likes. I don't know what she's looking for in a singer."

He smiled and steered the car into the club's small parking lot. "Neither do I. In fact, she doesn't even know she's looking for a singer. It should be quite a surprise."

He parked the car and walked around to help Temple out. He offered her his hand, and she felt shivers along her arm when his hand closed over hers.

Hastily, she pulled free of him and hoped he hadn't noticed.

"Has your friend ever had a singer here before?"

He drew his dark brows together and tipped his head thoughtfully to one side. "No. I don't think so."

Temple felt her nerves tighten more. "Suppose she refuses to hear me. I mean, if she's never hired a singer, she probably doesn't want one."

"She'll audition you as a favor to me. It's your job to make her interested."

They walked into the club, and the doorman greeted her companion with a wide smile. "Miss Weathers is right in here, Mr. St. James."

"Thank you, Adam."

Temple slowed her pace and examined the empty club. She made a quick count of the tables. Fifty. Maybe a few more. A bar ran the length of one wall, and directly in front of her was a small stage. A large yellow bird was painted on one wall, and miniature birds were carved into the wooden tables. She slid her suitcase between a table and the wall and waited.

Drops of perspiration tickled her skin and she took a few deep breaths to ward off the fear that was growing inside her.

Black curtains swished at one end of the stage and a woman stepped into view. She swept her long blond hair to one side and peered into the dark room. A smile curved her mouth.

"Zack! Why didn't you tell me you were coming?" She glided down the short flight of steps and closed the distance between them. Temple admired the green jumpsuit the woman wore and the graceful way she moved.

Zack held out his arms to her and the woman stood on tiptoe to kiss his cheek. Her green eyes darted in Temple's direction.

"Vivian Weathers, allow me to introduce Temple Anderson. She's here to audition as a singer."

Temple saw the woman open her mouth to object, but something in the man's expression stopped her. She swallowed and turned to Temple.

"You're a singer?"

"Yes, ma'am."

"Where have you appeared?"

Temple felt her courage sink to a new low. "I've . . ." She glanced at Zachary St. James, standing silently beside her, then continued. "I've sung at weddings and . . . parties."

The woman's penciled eyebrows rose. "That's all?"

"Yes," Temple whispered.

"Zack—really!" The woman shook her head. Zack touched her elbow.

"Excuse us, he said to Temple. "Vivian?" He led the woman to one dark corner of the room.

Temple strained to hear their conversation, but she couldn't catch any of their words. She closed her eyes and murmured a desperate prayer.

"Okay, honey." The woman's voice reached her from across the room.

Temple opened her eyes and saw Vivian Weathers motion for her to join them. Temple drew a shaking breath and crossed the room. The man's eyes glistened in the dim light and a faint smile touched the corners of his mouth. His confident air told her that the audition was set.

"Zack says you have some music with you." She turned back to the stage and called, "Marty!" The green eyes met Temple's again. "You give the song to Marty. I've got to check out the reservations for tonight; I'll be back in a few minutes and we'll see what you can do."

She turned to Zachary St. James and placed her hand in the crook of his arm.

"Come on, Zack. Let's give the little lady a chance to go over a few things with Marty."

"What do you want, Viv?"

Temple looked at the man on the stage. His auburn hair and freckled face bespoke good humor and his blue eyes seemed friendly.

"Oh, Marty. This little lady is going to audition for us; she sings. Help her work something up."

The woman nodded at Temple and led Zack to the back of the club.

"A singer, huh?"

Temple nodded and walked toward Marty. "Yes. I have some music here. Do you think you could help me select something appropriate?"

"Well, I'll try. I'm not really sure what would be appropriate here, though. We've never had a singer. I've been the only entertainment for seven years."

Temple examined him for a moment and wondered if he was irritated by her intrusion on his territory. "Can I be honest with you, Marty?"

He stuck his hands in his pockets and nodded. "Sure. I guess so."

Temple stepped close to him and lowered her voice. "I'm scared. Really terrified. This is my first real audition, and I need your help. I don't want to take anything away from you. I just need this job. I don't intend to settle in here. It's just a first step for me. Understand?"

His blue eyes met hers for a moment, and then he smiled. "Sure thing, kid. I understand. Let's see your music."

Temple exhaled in relief and handed him the tattered sheets. She twisted her hands and shifted her weight from one foot to the other as he scanned the music. Finally, he looked up and frowned. A new weakness ran through her as she took in his expression.

"What is it?" Temple stiffened her knees, hoping they wouldn't buckle.

"These songs are so old. Some of them date back to the thirties!"

27

"I know, but I like them. How about this one?" She took her favorite from the stack of music in his hands. "This is a good, bluesy song. Let's try it, okay?"

He shrugged and took the paper from her. "Okay," he said halfheartedly. He swept a drop cloth from a piano and sat on the bench. His eyes studied the notes and then he nodded. "Got it. You ready?"

Temple nodded and took two deep breaths. As the first notes broke through the silence she concentrated on her pitch and vocal control. Within a few bars she felt comfortable and she let the song flow through her and out into the empty club. She held the last note longer than usual, reveling in the way it seemed to bounce back to her from the walls.

Her voice trailed away into a long silence; then she heard Marty expel his breath in a soft whistle. She turned to him, eager to see his reaction.

"You're right, kid. That's a nice song, and you sure get every drop of life out of it."

Temple waited, then asked, "You mean it was okay?"

"Yes!" He stood up and patted her shoulder. "It was wonderful."

"I agree."

Temple whirled to find Vivian and Zack standing in the middle of the room. She felt her face burn, and her insides seemed to melt.

The woman moved closer. "Honey, do you think you could sing like that in front of a hundred people, or are you one of those who freeze up in front of an audience?"

"Yes! Yes, I can do it!" Temple tried to keep all the joy she felt from showing in her voice.

The woman nodded. "Come on down here, honey."

Temple left the stage and approached the woman she fervently hoped was about to become her new employer.

Vivian shook her hand, then handed her a white envelope. "Here's a week's salary. We'll take this a week at a time. I run a business, and if my customers don't go for you, you're out. No hard feelings. Now, you come back here tomorrow at one and rehearse with Marty. You'll open Friday night. Okay?"

Temple nodded, utterly speechless.

"Another thing, honey. You call me Vivian or Viv. Got it?"

Again Temple nodded. She looked toward Zachary St. James, the man who had become her benefactor, but couldn't make out his features in the dim room. Vivian followed her gaze.

"Stay around for a drink, Zack?"

"I'd like to, Viv, but I should take Miss Anderson to her . . ." He paused. "Hotel? Are you staying in a hotel, Miss Anderson?"

"Y-yes." Temple finally found her voice. She would take another room at the Mountain Top, she decided. At least she had a friend there now. "But, please, don't bother. I can call a cab. In fact, I have several errands to run, so please don't bother."

He moved into the light, and Temple was again struck by his magnetism.

"Very well, if you're sure."

"Yes, really. I'd rather."

"Let me call you a cab, then." He moved to one side, silently signaling her to precede him.

Before going, Temple turned to Vivian Weathers again. "Thank you for the audition, Miss . . . Vivian. It was nice meeting you. I'll be back tomorrow."

"Sure thing, honey."

Temple hurried from the room, picking up her things on the way and blinking quickly as she moved back into the bright afternoon sunlight. She felt Zack's presence behind her before he spoke.

"Ah, here's a cab." He held up two fingers and the cab braked to a stop in front of them.

Temple turned to him as he held the car door open for her. "Thank you, Mr. St. James. I wish I knew how to show my appreciation."

She regretted her choice of words immediately as his dark eyebrows lifted and his eyes glimmered with barely concealed amusement.

Before she could react, he took her hand and lifted it to his lips. The brief contact sent a hot current through her, leaving her lightheaded. He let her hand slip from his, then waited for her to climb into the taxi.

Temple was thankful for the cab's dark interior which hid her blush from his knowing eyes. The door slammed shut and she kept her eyes glued to the back of the driver's head. She only nodded in reply to Zack's whispered "Goodbye," not trusting herself to face him again.

The cab pulled away and the driver asked for her destination.

"Mountain Top Hotel," she murmured, still dazed by her final encounter with Zachary St. James.

She lowered her eyes to gaze at the back of her hand, half expecting to see a mark where his lips had touched. There was nothing, yet she was sure she could feel the warmth there.

She smoothed her fingertips slowly across the skin, then rubbed it vigorously, as if to wipe away the sensation.

I've never met anyone quite like him, she thought. The way he totally dominates his surroundings! And his eyes . . . so expressive, so strange. She wondered about his height. Probably several inches over six feet, she thought. In that black suit he would have seemed dark and brooding, sinister, even, if not for the light of life in his eyes.

Temple shook her head and fingered the white envelope. She hadn't even asked what her salary would be. She opened it and counted the money. Two hundred dollars! She felt her worries ease from her mind as she placed the bills in her purse. No more troubles, she thought. Not for a week, anyway. She smiled and thought of the letter she would write home.

Dear Mom and Dad,
   I've gotten a singing job in one of St.

Thomas's finest nightclubs. I'm making a good salary and I know I'll love the work. I have a wonderful boss named Vivian Weathers, a beautiful blonde with gorgeous green eyes. I think she's somewhere in her thirties. My piano player is named Marty. You'd like him. He's sweet, a real gentleman.

Temple paused in her imaginary letter and wondered if she should mention Zachary St. James. Should I tell them I've met an unbelievable man? A man who makes my blood race when I see him? A man who can make me giddy by just touching his lips to my hand? A man who seems to have the market cornered on male magnetism and charm?

She shook her head. No. They would think she'd gone mad. Besides, they would tell Jeremy and he would fly out here in a huff, demanding to know who this man was and if she was having an affair with him.

An affair? What would it be like to have an affair with a man like Zachary St. James? No. Not *like* Zachary St. James. It would have to *be* him, for surely no other man could be like him.

Temple allowed herself to get lost in the thought. He would be gentle. Generous in his lovemaking and . . .

Temple drew herself up with an audible gasp. What am I doing? she asked herself. I've barely even met the man. Of course, he's good-looking, and I *am* grateful to him, but this is getting ridiculous. Why, he probably has a wife and children!

The thought startled her. Was he married? Did he have children? Surely a man so attractive was married. Certainly he had a lover—or many, perhaps. Was Vivian his lover?

She recalled the possessive way Vivian had touched him. How her eyes had looked so familiarly at him.

She stopped herself again; this was no business of hers. And she had much more important things to think about than Zachary St. James's personal life. Her job, for instance; she would have to tell Scrappy all about it.

Her ears popped and she knew they were climbing to the hotel. She looked at her watch and realized that Scrappy would be off work now. She'd have to tell him the news tomorrow.

The cab stopped and Temple paid her fare, gathered her things together, and stepped out. At the hotel desk she booked a room, then took the elevator upstairs.

This room is too expensive, she thought as she looked around the pastel interior. I'll have to look for something more reasonable now that I'm staying on the island for a while.

She tossed her purse on the bed and started to hang her things in the closet. When she had finished, one evening dress hung among the more casual clothing. She examined the yellow gown and frowned. She would have to buy another one she decided. This one was too outdated. How long had she had it? She counted back. Three years. She nodded. Definitely time for a new one.

Temple ran some figures through her head. I'll pay my hotel bill and find an inexpensive room somewhere. Then, maybe, I'll have enough left over to buy a new evening gown.

Actually, she thought, I'll have to purchase several evening outfits if I stay on at the club. I can't wear the same thing every evening.

Temple closed the closet door and stretched out on the bed. The events of the day had drained her of energy, and she felt a pleasant lethargy steal over her.

I owe a lot to Zachary St. James, she told herself sleepily. He didn't have to be kind to me. Not after what I said about him.

His image floated behind her eyelids, and Temple sighed and let him weave his way into her dreams.

Chapter Two

Temple waited for the spotlight to fade before she exhaled and stumbled toward the red curtains that gave access to the backstage area. Once behind them, she leaned against the wall and closed her eyes, a smile on her lips.

"Nice show, honey."

Temple opened her eyes to find Vivian Weathers standing before her. On impulse Temple embraced the woman.

"Oh, Vivian! I'm so happy! They liked me, didn't they? Didn't they?"

Vivian's husky laugh brought another smile to Temple's lips. The woman disengaged herself gently and motioned toward the curtains.

"You heard them. You bet they liked you. That was a nice selection of songs. Just right."

"I can't take all the credit for that. Marty helped me. He's so wonderful. So kind."

Vivian nodded and patted her blond hair into place. "He is, that's for sure." Her green eyes moved over Temple. "Nice dress. Is it new?"

Temple glanced down at the ruby-red sequined gown with the crisscross bodice that left her back and shoulders bare. "Yes. I bought it yesterday. It's not too flashy?"

"Honey, flash and flair is what it's all about." Vivian placed a hand on Temple's arm. "I've got to get back out there. I just wanted to tell you that you added something special tonight. Keep it up."

"Thank you, Viv. Thank you." Temple blinked quickly to hide the sudden tears that filled her eyes.

Vivian smiled and left her, moving aside to let Marty by. He held out his arms and hugged Temple to him. He laughed. "Kid, you knocked them over!"

Temple laughed, too, and held Marty closer, then moved back to look at his face.

"Thanks to you, Marty. I can't thank you enough for . . ."

"No, wait!" he interrupted her. "*You* worked that magic out there, kid. Don't think for a minute that anyone helped you. When that spotlight hit you, you were on your own." He kissed the tip of her nose. "Well, I've got to go and play more music. By the way, you look terrific tonight. Smashing."

Temple watched him disappear between the folds of the draperies. She leaned back against the wall, postponing the time when she would remove her dress and replace it with street clothes. The dress seemed to be part of the evening's magic, and she wasn't ready for the spell to be broken.

She could hear the murmur of the crowd and

the faint notes of the piano. She moved toward the curtains and parted them slightly to peek out at the customers. Such wonderful people, she thought. Do they know how happy they've made me tonight? Do they know they're responsible for helping me realize my dream?

Her gaze moved over the unfamiliar faces until it was arrested by a pair of dark eyes. She caught her breath when she saw the dancing lights in the black pupils.

"Zachary St. James." The name slipped through her parted lips.

He held up a hand and motioned for her to join him.

Should I act as if I didn't see him? she wondered. No, that would be rude. After all, he's responsible for my being here.

She stood up straighter and sucked in her breath before she left the concealing darkness. As she neared him, he stood and held out the other chair for her.

"Allow me to buy you a drink, Miss Anderson."

She nodded and sat down. He gestured for a waiter before he joined her. "What's your pleasure?"

"I'll just have orange juice, please."

He frowned and shook his head. "Nonsense! A performance such as the one you gave tonight deserves something much more pleasant." He turned to the waiter. "Let's have a bottle of champagne, Frederick. The best you have to offer."

"Very good, Mr. St. James." The waiter bowed and left them.

Zachary leaned back in his chair, his gaze resting on Temple's face for a few moments before he spoke. "I believe you said your home is in San Juan?"

"Yes, that's right."

"Were you born there?"

"No. My family lives in New York."

"Ah!" He reached into the pocket of his dark suit jacket and withdrew a thin silver case. The lid popped open at his touch and he offered her a cigarette.

"No, thank you."

"Do you mind if I smoke?"

At the shake of her head, he withdrew one of the cigarettes and placed it between his full lips. He reached for the candle in the center of the table and touched the flame to the tip of the cigarette.

Temple watched the flame as it was reflected in his dark eyes. The glow seemed to rest there, even when he placed the candle back onto the table.

"So"—he exhaled the smoke—"you came to St. Thomas to find your . . . fortune?"

Temple lifted her chin and met his taunting eyes. "No. To find my independence."

A dark eyebrow rose at her statement. "And have you?"

"In a way—yes."

"This—independence—is important to you?"

"Yes. I don't want to have to depend on anyone else."

One corner of his mouth rose slightly and he tipped his head to one side in a thoughtful

38

gesture. His voice was low, his speech slow and deliberate. "But we must always depend on others. We depend on other people to make us happy, to encourage and support us. Other people to . . . love us."

Temple felt mesmerized by his words. She tried to think of something to say in reply but could find nothing with which to counter his argument or explain what she had meant.

The waiter returned with a bottle of champagne resting in a bucket of crushed ice. He opened the bottle carefully and poured a small measure of the golden liquid into a glass which he extended toward Zachary.

Zachary tasted the champagne and nodded. "Yes, that's a nice choice. Thank you, Frederick."

The waiter poured a glass of the bubbly liquid for Temple, then refilled Zachary's glass. He replaced the bottle in the bucket and moved away.

Zachary lifted his glass. "A toast. May there be many more nights of song . . . for both of us."

Temple hesitated before sipping, letting his toast register in her mind. When she did taste it, the champagne was dry and full of flavor, and she wondered if it was terribly expensive.

Over the rim of her glass she caught sight of Vivian. The woman was watching her, a worried expression on her face.

Zachary turned in his chair to follow Temple's gaze. When he faced Temple again, he was smiling. "Vivian is wise to me." He sipped the champagne. "She knows my intentions toward you are strictly dishonorable." His smile widened in response to her startled look. He leaned forward until his breath touched her cheek. "It is up to you to make my intentions honorable."

Temple moved away from him until her back met the chair. What on earth was he talking about? Her breath came in short gasps and her lips moved, though no words were forthcoming.

"Zack! Dear, dear Zack!"

He looked up and then stood quickly when he saw the woman who had addressed him. Temple took a deep breath and studied the newcomers. The woman, who seemed to be in her thirties, had a round, wholesome face. Her light brown hair was straight and shoulder-length, and her eyes were a deep gold. She rested her hands on Zack's shoulders, pulling him down so that she could kiss his cheek.

The man behind her was older, perhaps forty. His hair was blond and thinning, and his eyes were a bright sky blue. He pumped Zack's hand, and lines fanned from the corners of his eyes when he smiled.

"William, Mary, allow me to introduce Miss Anderson. Temple, Dr. and Mrs. Eustes."

The man spoke. "Please, Mary and William. We're honored, Miss Anderson. We heard you sing and we were both quite impressed."

"You were marvelous!" The woman gave Temple a smile.

Temple blushed at the compliments. "Thank you. Please, call me Temple."

"Does that include me, too?" Zachary questioned her, a teasing glint in his dark eyes.

Temple felt the color in her cheeks deepen, and she nodded.

"Good! And from now on I'm Zack. William, Mary, won't you join us for some champagne?"

As they settled into seats Zachary chose one close to Temple. She resisted the urge to move away. She could smell the musky scent of his aftershave lotion, and his elbow resting against hers seemed to send an electric current through her arm.

She made an effort to concentrate on the conversation, trying to ignore the variety of feelings that were stirring in her.

"Have you been out on your yacht lately?" William was asking now.

"Yes; in fact, I just returned from St. Croix a few days ago."

As he spoke he was pouring more champagne into Temple's glass. She started to protest, but Zachary shook his head.

"The champagne is in your honor. Enjoy it."

"Are you from the islands?" Mary asked.

Temple tore her eyes from Zachary's and answered, "No. I'm from the States, but I've been living in San Juan the last few years. I've only been in St. Thomas a short time."

"Well, you've made quite a splash!" Mary told her. "You're quite talented."

"Thank you. Do you live on St. Thomas?"

"Yes. William has a practice here. Oh! Zack, did I tell you?" Mary touched Zack's arm and her eyes twinkled. "Candice is coming back to the island next week. Or did you already know?"

Zack shook his head. "No. I hadn't heard."

"That woman!" William frowned good-naturedly. "She's been as restless as a butterfly ever since she inherited that money from her grandfather."

"Well, she's young," Mary protested. "Why shouldn't she have fun? There will be plenty of time later for her to settle down."

Temple turned her eyes in Zachary's direction and saw the polite smile that had settled on his face as he listened to Mary. Who is Candice? she wondered. An old flame of Zachary's? She longed to ask, but she quashed the urge. It's none of my business, she thought.

"Won't you join us, Temple?"

Temple turned bewildered eyes to Zachary's face. What? She cleared her throat. "I'm sorry. What did you say?"

"You still have stardust in your mind, eh?" He smiled at her, his teeth showing white in the dim light. "I asked if you'd like to join us at a restaurant for a light dinner?"

"No. I—I'm rather tired. I think I'll go home. Thank you, anyway." She looked toward the stage area, suddenly anxious to change her clothes and leave.

"Very well. Have you a car?"

"I . . . no. I'll take a taxi home."

"Go change your clothes, and I'll have Andrew drive you home. I'll leave with Mary and William; Andrew can pick me up later at the restaurant."

"Andrew?"

He nodded. "Andrew is my man Friday."

"I don't think—"

"That's right," he said as he stood and positioned himself behind her chair, "don't think. Just accept my offer."

She shrugged off any further protests and said her goodbyes. Quickly she left and went to her dressing room, where she changed into a cream-colored dress with a pleated skirt and then made her way to the club entrance.

Zachary was waiting for her outside. A man dressed in a dark suit and white shirt stood beside him.

"Ah, here she is. Temple, this is Andrew."

The man swept a short-brimmed hat from his head and bowed slightly from the waist. "Hello, miss."

"Andrew, take the lady home, then meet me at the restaurant. Okay?"

"Yes, sir." Andrew replaced his hat and opened the rear door of a white Mercedes. "Miss?"

Temple climbed into the back seat and Andrew shut the door. Zachary leaned forward, and Temple rolled the glass down so she could hear him.

"I just wanted to say goodnight and to thank you for the lovely evening." His eyes sparkled in the moonlight.

Temple started to thank him for the use of his car, but the words died in her throat when his forefinger curled under her chin, lifting it so that his lips brushed hers. He stopped and looked into her eyes; then his lips settled on hers again, passionate and demanding.

The warmth of his mouth on hers sent a spark

of fire through her, and even when he moved away from her she felt her lips burn. She wet them with the tip of her tongue and met his dark gaze. His eyes held hers for several seconds; then he turned and walked back into the club.

"Miss? Where would you like to go?"

Temple tore her eyes away from the door through which Zack had vanished and returned her attention to Andrew. She murmured the address and then settled back in the seat, her eyes focused on nothing in particular as Andrew gracefully maneuvered the big car through the dark streets.

Her lips still felt warm when her tongue touched them. Why do I react this way to him? she wondered. It had been such a brief kiss, yet something had stirred in her, something quite different from her reactions to the other kisses she had known.

"Have you worked for Mr. St. James long, Andrew?"

"I've been with him fifteen years, miss."

"That long?" Temple hesitated, then asked, "Are you with him when he's on his yacht?"

"I always go with him, miss."

"Oh, I see." She looked out the window and saw the small apartment building where she was now living come into view. She gathered her things together and realized that she would learn no more about Zachary St. James tonight.

"Thank you, Andrew," she said as he stopped the car and opened the door for her.

"You're welcome, miss. Miss, how long did you live in San Juan?"

"Three years. . . . How did you know I lived there?"

He smiled. "Mr. St. James told me. I have relatives in San Juan."

"Oh. . . . Well, thank you again. Goodnight."

"Good evening, miss."

As Temple waited for the elevator a few moments later, she wondered at the thrill she felt.

"So, he talked about me to Andrew?" she whispered to herself. "I wonder what else he said about me?"

The elevator doors slid open and Temple touched her lips with her fingertips as she entered. I wonder if he's talked about me to anyone else? She smothered a giggle. Quit acting like a ninny, she thought. Still, she couldn't erase the smile that curved her lips.

She entered the club and thought how familiar it seemed to her now. The large yellow birds spread their wings along the walls and lifted her spirits even higher.

"Temple, could I speak to you for a few minutes?" Vivian rounded the bar and approached Temple. "Let's have a glass of juice, hmmm?"

Temple nodded and watched as Vivian poured fresh golden orange juice into two glasses. As always, Vivian looked lovely. The chic black suit accented her fair complexion and wheat-colored hair.

"Here we are. Have a seat, honey." Vivian nodded to the table near Temple.

Temple slipped into one of the chairs and

crossed her fingers, hoping Vivian wasn't going to fire her.

"Is something wrong, Vivian? Last night you—"

A husky laugh grew in Vivian's throat. "No, no, honey. Don't look so worried. I'm not going to fire you." She took a drink, then settled back in her chair, a smile still on her lips. "I just want to have a woman-to-woman talk with you."

A tingle of apprehension touched Temple's spine and her mouth felt suddenly dry. She sipped at the tangy orange juice and waited.

"I was watching you last night with Zachary."

Temple sighed. "Vivian, there's nothing between Zachary and me. I hardly know him and—"

"Well, I *do* know him, and I know that look that was on your face last night. I've had that look myself. I'm not accusing you of anything, honey. I just want you to be cautious."

"I think you're being premature, Vivian." Temple tried to make her tone light, ignoring the feeling of dread that was coursing through her. "I haven't said more than a few words to him. Last night he was just being a gentleman and buying me a drink to celebrate my opening here."

"Oh, yes, he can be a gentleman—when he wants to be. In fact, he can be almost anything to anyone when it suits him." Vivian smiled and finished her drink. "Did he tell you that he owns this club?"

Temple blinked at the other woman and felt her mouth drop open.

Vivian's smile grew. "He didn't, huh? Well, he owns it, and I manage it. Zachary owns several businesses in this area. I admire him. He's only thirty-seven and he's a self-made millionaire. Why, I've known Zack . . ." Vivian lifted her green eyes to the ceiling for a moment. "Fifteen years! Before he even knew that Giselle existed."

"Giselle?" Temple prompted.

"Yes, his wife."

A pain stabbed Temple's heart and she closed her eyes for a second. He *is* married, she thought, and a new shaft of pain found its way through her.

"He's . . . married." Temple heard her voice quaver.

"He was. He's a widower."

"A widower," Temple echoed. Relief rushed through her, and she felt guilty at the strength of her reaction.

"Yes. Giselle died in a plane crash a year ago. You really don't know very much about Zack, do you?"

Temple managed to laugh. "How could I? Viv, I just met him a couple of days ago. That's why this whole conversation is so silly."

Vivian shook her head and the light shimmered in her hair. "Not when we're talking about Zachary St. James."

"Look, Viv," Temple said, leaning forward and resting her arms on the tabletop, "if you're telling me that you and Zack are a twosome . . . I understand."

Vivian shook her head again, and her eyes

sparkled with humor. "That's not what I'm talking about, honey. Oh, Zack and I have had our flings." A misty expression touched her face. "At one time—before Giselle—I thought that . . ." The expression vanished and she shrugged her shoulders. "Never mind that. It's history. Nowadays we're just good friends and he plays the field, although Candice might not agree with that statement." Vivian looked past Temple. "Sam! Can we have a refill on this juice?"

Sam nodded and came over to fill their empty glasses. Again Temple found herself wondering about Candice. She must be important to Zack, or why would his friends keep mentioning her? Yet he hadn't even known she was coming back to the island.

When Sam had returned to the bar, Vivian shifted in her seat and sighed deeply. "Giselle was my sister."

The sentence seemed to hang in the air between them.

"She came to the islands to visit me. She'd been through a messy divorce and wanted to get away from the States for a while." Vivian's voice was low, and Temple found herself leaning closer to her in order to catch each word.

"I had been dating Zack, and then he bought this club and asked me to manage it." Her green eyes lifted to focus on Temple. "He's terribly generous. Anyway, Giselle met him, and it was obvious from the start that she meant to have him. She was a very impulsive person—very determined. Within two months they were planning their wedding. Things moved very fast, but that's how Giselle worked. She had no patience."

"And she died in a plane crash. How awful for you." Temple rested her hand on Vivian's in a comforting gesture.

"Yes. It hit both of us very hard." Vivian sighed. "But that's not what I want to talk to you about. Temple, honey, I just don't want you to get hurt. I know how seductive Zack can be."

Temple found herself nodding in agreement before she caught herself. "Viv, don't worry. He's not interested in me."

"Ha!" Vivian tossed her head and laughed. "That's how much you know! I saw the two of you last night. Believe me, he's zeroing in on you."

Temple found herself feeling a bit bewildered. "But you mentioned Candice."

"Oh, Candice." Vivian gave a dismissive shrug. "Mary and William have been pushing Candice into Zack's arms, but I'm not so sure he's interested—especially now that he's met you."

Temple's heart pounded against her rib cage at the thought. Could it be true? Was Zachary really interested in her?

"Honey, wipe that wistful look off your face," Vivian warned. "Don't get me wrong. Zack's a wonderful man, but you're biting off more than you can chew. There's a lot you should know about him before you decide to accept his attentions."

"Like what?" Temple questioned. "What should I know?"

Vivian shook her head. "It's not my business to discuss. That information will have to come from Zack." She pointed a long fingernail at Temple. "You just beware. Think, before you let that heart of yours take the lead."

Temple smiled, trying to look a lot more secure than she felt. "It's nice of you to be concerned, Viv, but I'm not a child. I've been around."

Vivian raised her penciled brows and gave Temple a skeptical look.

Temple colored and laughed. "Well, I've been around people who've been around, and I'm a good listener." She raised her chin. "I *do* know how to take care of myself."

Vivian smiled. "I'm sure you do, honey. But Zack isn't your ordinary man. You'll need all the experience and know-how you can muster to keep him at arm's length." Vivian squeezed Temple's hand. "Go on, get dressed. Lecture's over. But if you ever want to talk, just come to me. I'm a good listener, too."

Temple smiled at the other woman and retreated to her tiny dressing room. The dress she had worn the night before hung in the closet next to a second dress, which she pulled from the hanger and held up against her. She spun toward the mirror and examined herself. The jade-green material had a metallic sheen to it; the dress was cut off the shoulder and the hem fell just below her knees. Her fingers slid over the wide band of silver that shimmered at the waist. She recalled how that band of silver accented her narrow waist, and the memory brought a smile to her lips.

The smile froze when her gaze drifted to the pedestal table. Atop the table stood a vase filled with the rich red blossoms of the royal poinciana.

A white card dangled in the midst of the fiery blooms and Temple examined the bold handwriting.

Now that you're part of the island, please wear the island's flower. Zack.

Temple let the card slip from her trembling fingers. She bent nearer to the blooms and breathed in their aroma. She remembered seeing the umbrella-shaped trees that bore these blooms scattered all across the island.

She glanced at her wristwatch and sighed. Time to get dressed, she told herself as she moved away from the vase of scarlet flowers, purposely pushing thoughts of Zachary St. James from her mind.

As the applause died in her ears, Temple slipped into her dressing room and breathed a sigh of relief. Another show over, and the audience still liked her! She smiled and slid out of the jade-colored dress. She traded the dress for a pair of white slacks and a red tube top. As she gathered her belongings, her eyes slid over to the vase of flowers.

I'll leave them here to add color to my dressing room, she thought. Then she plucked one of the red blooms from a slender branch and tucked it behind her ear. She bent and looked at the effect

51

in the makeup mirror. The flower matched her top and made a brilliant splash of color in her dark hair. Her blue eyes sparkled as she quickly added a deep pink lip gloss to her full lips, then moved away from her image and toward the door that led to the alley. Outside, the tropical breeze kissed her moist skin and she walked quickly toward the street, anxious to find a cab to take her back to her new apartment. Her heart skipped a beat when she saw a shadow detach itself from the larger shadow of the building.

"Good evening, Temple."

His voice caused her heart to tumble over itself. "Hello, Zack."

In a few long strides he was by her side. "I see you received my flowers."

She touched the bloom near her cheek. "Yes, thank you. They're lovely."

"They suit you."

He had moved to stop in front of her, and she could see the dark glitter of his eyes. He was so near that she could feel the warmth of his breath on her face.

"Heading home?" He waited for her nod. "I'll take you, but first I hope you won't mind joining me for a nightcap."

It wasn't a question, so he didn't wait for her response. His hand curled around her elbow and he propelled her toward the street where the Mercedes stood waiting.

"You remember Andrew, don't you?" He held the car door open for her and nodded toward the figure behind the steering wheel.

Temple shrugged off the protest that dangled on her tongue and smiled at Andrew as she climbed into the back seat.

"Andrew, let's go to the Tropics Club." He turned toward her. "Have you been there?"

"No. I haven't had time to visit very many places or do much sightseeing."

"Of course. I think you'll like this club. It's very quiet. Very private."

Something in his voice brought her eyes to his face. A smile tugged at the corners of his mouth as he reached into his jacket for a cigarette. The flame from his lighter sent a glow washing over his face, and Temple thought how strong and clean-lined that face appeared in the brief second that it was illuminated.

"I thought that the club would provide us with the atmosphere we need."

Temple stared at him for a moment, watching the smoke escape through his full lips. "Atmosphere? For what?"

He smiled, his teeth showing white in the dark interior of the car. "I'd like to know you better, and it seems we're always interrupted. Like last night. Even though I enjoyed seeing William and Mary, I was disappointed when you refused to join us for a late dinner."

"I was tired. I enjoyed meeting your friends, though. They seem like a nice couple."

"I've always thought so."

The automobile glided to a stop at the curb. Temple looked up at the building before her. Not a skyscraper, but taller than most of the buildings on the island.

"The club is upstairs on the top floor." Zack turned to Andrew, who was holding the car door open for them. "Thank you, Andrew. You can collect us in a couple of hours."

"But I—" Temple started to protest, but Zack's fingertip touched her lips, halting her words. She pulled back from him and swallowed, trying to still the pulse that beat in her throat.

"Let's not argue. You don't have to report for work until midafternoon tomorrow. Let's enjoy a few quiet hours." He paused. "Together."

His voice was like velvet, and Temple could not muster an argument. She stepped from the car and tried not to jump when his hand rested against the small of her back. She stopped and turned to him.

"I'm—I'm not dressed for a fancy club. I shouldn't . . ."

His mocking eyes bore into hers. "Always worried about your clothes, aren't you?" He stepped back and his eyes moved over her, seeming to strip her where she stood. "You look lovely. Lovely."

Temple stood rooted as his dark gaze traveled back down from her face to linger on her exposed shoulders, then down the length of her body. Her skin burned as if his gaze were more—as if it were his hands that were exploring the curves of her body.

His hand moved to capture hers, and she stumbled after him toward the elevator. She took a deep breath and tried to shake the feeling of being hypnotized by this man and his glistening gaze.

Chapter Three

The cream-colored pants, vest, and shirt and the chocolate-brown tie and jacket seemed to add even more virility to the man, Temple thought, as her eyes moved over him where he sat opposite her.

Tearing her gaze from him, she glanced around the large room. Because of the dense foliage that surrounded the alcove she couldn't see very much of the club. On their arrival, the waiter had immediately taken them to this secluded corner of the room. She sighed and nestled more deeply into the spacious leather chair.

"You don't like the club?"

His resonant voice set her nerves humming again. "No! The club is lovely. Really."

A chuckle rumbled deep in his throat, and his dark eyes sparkled. "Don't worry; I believe you. What would you like to drink?"

"I'll have a glass of white wine, please."

His dark head nodded and he motioned for the waiter. "A glass of white wine for the lady, and I'll have Scotch and water, please."

"Very good, Mr. St. James."

Temple watched the man move away from the table and wondered if everyone on the island knew Zachary St. James. The thought lit a fuse inside her, and she turned back to her companion. "Do you own this club, too?"

His intense gaze narrowed a fraction. "No. Why do you ask?"

"Because Vivian told me today that you own the Yellowbird. Why didn't you just tell her to hire me and dispense with my audition?"

His mouth twisted in displeasure at her sharp tone, but he kept his voice level. "Vivian runs that club as she sees fit. I rarely interfere."

"But you did this time, didn't you?"

"If you're asking whether or not I told Viv to hire you, the answer is no."

Temple crossed her legs at the knees and smiled confidently. "But of course you wouldn't have to insist, would you? All you'd have to do is make a suggestion, and Viv wouldn't dare disobey. After all, you're her boss."

Her comments brought only another chuckle, not the anger she had expected, and Temple felt her own anger rise.

"Obviously you don't know Vivian, or you'd realize how foolish that statement is. Viv doesn't have to listen to me. That was one of the ground rules she insisted on when she assumed the management of the club. She runs it; I don't interfere."

The waiter suddenly appeared at Zack's elbow, placing their drinks on the table. Zack lifted his glass in an ironic salute, his eyes still locked on Temple. Suddenly her mouth felt dry and she sipped nervously at the wine. Refusing to let him think she had been taken in by his smooth answers and ready explanations, Temple decided to have the last word.

"Regardless of how strong-minded Vivian may be, I know you're not the kind of man one says no to very easily."

Slowly he placed his glass on the table. His lashes lifted so that his ebony eyes could meet her blue ones. "I'm glad you find me so irresistible."

"I didn't say—" She bit off the end of the protest when she saw the mocking grin curving his mouth.

He laughed and quickly finished his drink. Temple tensed as his hand covered hers and he pulled her to her feet.

"Come on, let me show you some of beautiful St. Thomas. The island is as lovely at night as it is during the day. I don't think there's any reason for us to stay here, after all."

"But Andrew won't be back yet."

He paused at the club entrance to tuck some bills in the maître d's hand. "If I know Andrew, he'll be parked right outside, waiting for us." He placed his fingertips against the small of her back, and Temple hurried toward the elevator. She longed to escape his touch, however light it might be. When he touched her, she suddenly had no will of her own, and the feeling alarmed her.

Outside, Andrew stepped quickly from the car and opened the door for them. She caught Zack's knowing wink but ignored him.

"Andrew, let's show the lady some of our island, shall we? Just cruise along and let us soak up some scenery."

"Yes, sir. Would the lady like to see Drake's Seat?"

"Drake's Seat?" Temple echoed.

"Yes," Zack said, answering for her. Then, leaning forward, he flipped a switch, and a smoked-glass panel slid up to separate Andrew from them. Temple gave a shocked gasp and turned to Zack.

"Not that he eavesdrops, but I do like my privacy, you understand."

Temple swallowed. "Surely there's nothing you'd say to me that Andrew couldn't hear."

He smiled and settled back against the seat, only inches separating them. Temple quelled the urge to squeeze closer to the door, unwilling to let him know how much his nearness affected her.

"Oh, I might be tempted to say something that would be for your ears only. After all, the moon is full and the stars are afire. Those things tend to have a strange effect on a man."

Temple let out a shaky laugh. "You sound like the Wolfman or—or Dracula!"

The dark gaze swept her face, lingered on her throat, and then found her mouth. "Perhaps I am a bit of both. Hmmm?" The last was merely a low growl, deep in his throat.

A shiver snaked up Temple's spine, and she chided herself inwardly for being such a fool. Forcing her eyes away from his, she stared out the window and tried to concentrate on the deserted streets of Charlotte Amalie, the island's capital. Andrew was driving along a winding road that led up one of the island's steepest mountains. Wisps of bougainvillea tapped against the window as Andrew steered the car so that it hugged the side of the road to miss a few uncaring goats.

"So, you and Viv were talking about me today?"

Temple kept her eyes on the passing scenery. "Yes. That's right."

"What else did she tell you about me?"

"Nothing much."

"I find that hard to believe, since she knows so much about me. We've been friends for some time."

"Yes. You're her brother-in-law."

She heard his swift intake of breath, but she didn't turn to see his expression.

"Ah, so you talked of Giselle."

"Yes. I'm sorry for . . ."

"Don't be." His tone was brusque. "I've had enough people offering their sympathy. I'm tired of it."

His cold voice made Temple turn her head. His expression was taciturn. She sighed and resumed her sightseeing. The car was slowing, gradually coming to a halt before a short retaining wall. Temple's eyes widened as she caught the breathtaking view of the sea over Andrew's shoulder.

"Oh, my!" She strained forward in her seat, trying to get a better view. "It's—it's lovely."

"You can see it better if we get out of the car."

Zack reached behind her to open the door. The warm sea breeze stole into the car and Temple breathed in the aroma of a thousand blossoms. She stepped from the confines of the automobile and crossed to the retaining wall. The sea pitched and rolled, and a gust of wind tousled her hair. Temple smiled and tilted her head back, glorying in the smell of the salty sea and the breath of the wind on her skin.

A warmer breath touched her cheek. She darted a look to her left to find Zack standing near her.

"Don't you want to see Drake's Seat?"

"Isn't this it?"

He smiled, and Temple thought how attractive that smile was—the way the tiny lines fanned out from the corners of his eyes and the way those eyes seemed to soften into velvet.

"No. This is Magens Bay, and Hans Lollick Island is off that way." He pointed to the northeast as he spoke. "Drake's Seat is behind us. Come on." His hand closed over hers and he gently pulled her away from the view of the sea. As they passed the car, Temple turned to see that Andrew had remained in the front seat.

She came to an abrupt halt as she ran into Zachary's broad back. Straightening, she mumbled an apology, which he seemed scarcely to hear.

"There. That's Drake's Seat."

Temple looked up and in the bright starlight saw a pink stone seat nestled against a backdrop of green foliage. It was massive, a couch carved from stone.

"My goodness! What's it for?"

He guided her toward a flight of steps that led up to the seat. "It was made for Sir Francis Drake. He could sit here looking out to sea, keeping watch for enemy ships."

"Oh, how romantic!"

"Romantic?" He tossed his dark head and laughed. "He destroyed the enemy ships he spotted. I don't think *they* thought he was very romantic."

Temple slapped at him playfully, then sat on the cool bench, her eyes fastened on the sea. "You know what I mean. That whole period seems so romantic. Those were the days of pirates and swashbucklers. Of maidens kidnaped by ruthless men."

Temple stiffened suddenly as she felt him sit close beside her, his hard thigh pressed against her own. She kept her gaze on the sea, even though she felt a compelling urge to face him.

His breath fanned her cheek when he spoke, "And would you think it was romantic if a swashbuckler kidnaped you?"

Temple hated the way her attempt at a laugh trembled into nothingness. "N-no. I'd probably be scared to death!"

"I should think you'd scratch and claw like a wild thing," he whispered.

Temple felt him move toward her, and she sucked in her breath as she felt his warm mouth touch her bare shoulder. His lips moved along her skin, then glided up her neck. She trembled when his moist mouth found pleasure points she had never known she possessed.

One strong arm stole about her waist, and Temple rested weakly against him. Somewhere in the back of her mind she realized that she had been waiting for this moment. Waiting for this man to touch her, to kiss her, to hold her as he was doing now.

Suddenly impatient to make the dream a reality, Temple sighed. Zachary's lips at once found hers, taking them up on their silent offer.

The mastery of his kiss overwhelmed Temple. Never had she been kissed with such surety— such purpose. Of their own accord her hands slipped through his thick brown hair, and his kiss deepened, taking the last of her breath away. Temple's head began to spin as his insistent lips continued to probe and tease her.

When she thought that she might faint at the passion this man was raising within her, he suddenly lifted his mouth from hers. His face was poised above hers, inches away, and she could smell his aftershave, mixed with his own masculine fragrance. The aroma added to the intoxication she felt.

A smile curved his full lips. "Thank you for not scratching me, little wildcat." His eyes devoured her for several moments. "Ah! Those eyes. As deep and as mysterious as the sea. How I love to drink of their power."

Her heart soared along with her emotions as he again claimed her lips. Temple felt a wanton urge sweep through her and responded to his kiss with all her being. Wrapping her arms about his strong neck, she let her fingers discover the strength in his shoulders and back.

Slowly he moved his mouth from her lips and pressed swift kisses along the column of her throat. When the stiffened tip of his tongue touched the sensitive skin between her breasts, Temple became aware of her own ragged breathing—and of something else. An arousal and need for fulfillment she had never known before.

When his questing fingers touched the curve of her breasts, something cold and reasoning stirred in Temple. Cool caution began to fight the hot passion within her, and she stirred and pushed gently, almost regretfully, at his shoulders.

Reluctantly he moved away, but his eyes still held her in their grasp. "It is inevitable, little wildcat. Can't you see?" His voice was a caress. "You will be mine. I knew it when I first saw you."

Temple struggled for control. She straightened on the stone seat and tore her gaze away from his. "I—I think we should go now. I want to go home."

He laughed softly. "You don't *want* to go home—you just think you *should* go home." His hand found her flushed cheek and he forced her to face him. "There is a difference, Temple." His mouth brushed hers again. "You will be mine, Temple. In fact, you are already, aren't you?"

"I—I don't know what you're talking about." Temple averted her gaze and tried to control the trembling she felt within her. She knew this man could arouse her as no other man, certainly not Jeremy, had ever done. But that had nothing to do with belonging to someone, with loving him. Vivian's words came back to haunt her, and she steeled herself against Zack's powerful magnetism.

"You know exactly what I mean. I *will* have you." He smiled and stood, pulling her to her feet. "We will go now. But just remember, Temple"—his strong fingers gripped her shoulders and his gaze arrested hers—"we are bound to each other as surely as the shore is bound to the sea."

Chapter Four

Temple unplugged the vacuum cleaner, glanced around the spotless living room, and smiled. She put the vacuum in the closet and dropped into a chair. Dangling one leg over the arm, she wondered what to do with herself for the rest of the day.

She supposed she could go shopping, or read the novel she'd picked up the other day. Neither suggestion sounded interesting, though, and she sighed and traced the flowered pattern of the material with her fingertip. Her thoughts floated to Zack, as they had done constantly for almost a week, and she wondered why she hadn't heard from him.

After that evening at Drake's Seat she had tossed restlessly for hours before falling asleep to dream of him. He had sounded so sure of himself, so sinister, when he'd told her that he meant to have her. She knew how attracted to him she was, and that he was equally attracted to her wasn't in doubt, but the thought that he meant to control her, to do with her what he wanted, scared her. She tried to tell herself that she was glad he hadn't called her, that he'd apparently changed his mind, yet her heart persisted in feeling disappointment, hurt that she hadn't heard from him again.

She jumped at the light tap on her door. Her eyes sparkled. It was him; she was sure of it. She flung open the door, then stifled a gasp.

"Jeremy! What on earth are you doing here?"

She stared at him, unwilling to believe her eyes. He looked just the same. Same blond hair. Same dark blue eyes. Same sensible blue suit. Same Jeremy.

"Won't you ask me in?"

He sounded tense, strained. Temple stood aside to let him pass. He glanced around, then focused his eyes on her.

"I have to talk to you. Why don't you close the door?"

Temple swallowed and shut the door. "Have a seat, Jeremy. Why didn't you call and tell me you were coming?"

He shrugged and sat down on the sofa. "I didn't think you'd object to my coming to see you."

Temple sat in the armchair. "No, I don't object. I—I'm just surprised."

He rested his arm along the sofa's back. "So, how do you like your job?"

"Oh, it's very exciting, but . . ." Temple let the sentence trail off. She shifted and wondered why she suddenly felt so uncomfortable with Jeremy.

"But what?"

"Oh, it's just not as easy as I'd thought. I

mean, it's hard to make myself sing night after night. Sometimes I just don't feel like it, and sometimes the audience isn't very attentive."

"In a way, I'm glad to hear that."

Temple felt the old resentment flood through her. So! He thinks I'm ready to give it all up and fly back home with him, she thought. That's why he's here, to get me to leave. She squared her shoulders and looked him straight in the eye. "What does that mean, Jeremy?"

He ran a hand through his straight hair. "It just means that now I feel better about the request I'm going to make. I want you to come back home, Temple."

"No!" She rose from the chair. "I love it here. I'm not going back. Did Mom and Dad put you up to this, or is it all your idea?"

"Your parents don't even know that I'm here. I came in their behalf, however."

Something in his voice cut through Temple's anger. She balled her hands at her sides and asked, "Is something wrong? Jeremy? Mom and Dad—are they . . . ?"

"They're in a financial bind, Temple. It's pretty bad, I'm afraid."

Her knees gave way and she sat in the chair. "How bad?"

Jeremy frowned, as if he didn't want to tell her. "Your father made some investments, and the man skipped with the money. The guy was a real smoothy; he took half a dozen people in. He took virtually all of your father's savings, plus everything he could borrow, and promised to double or triple the amount through invest-ments. Instead, he left the country." Jeremy sighed and gazed at the ashtray on the table in front of him. "He's going to have to sell his business, Temple."

"Oh, no!" Temple's hands fluttered to her face. "No, it can't be! Surely something can be done, Jeremy!"

"Don't you think I've investigated every angle? There's no alternative."

"Can't they borrow more money?"

Jeremy shook his head. "That would only com-plicate matters. Besides, the amount is too large. No one will lend them that kind of money, not with the other loans already outstanding."

"H-how much money, Jeremy?"

The figure he named drained the color from Temple's face, and she leaned back in the chair. "That much?" Her voice was a whisper.

"Yes. That's why you need to come home. Your parents need you near them now. They need your support, Temple." Jeremy stood and crossed to her. His fingers gripped her shoul-ders. "Come home, Temple. Your place is with them."

Temple rested her cheek on his hand and stared at the bay window. Her world seemed to be falling apart around her. I don't want to leave, she thought. But what else can I do?

"Let me think, Jeremy. Maybe I can find a way—"

"Temple, for once in your life, be sensible! I've researched the possibilities. Come home!"

"Quit telling me what to do!" Temple pulled from his grasp and went to stand by the window. "I have a life, too! I need to think this out. . . . I'll talk to Vivian. She might have a suggestion."

"Vivian? That woman at the club?"

Temple turned to face him. "You've met her?"

He nodded and walked to her side. "I went to the club to find out your address. What on earth do you think she can do?"

"I don't know. She knows some important people. Maybe—"

"Maybe nothing!" He grabbed her arm and turned her to face him, fastening his blue eyes on her. His face was set, his expression grim. "Temple, when are you going to grow up?"

Temple stiffened and narrowed her eyes. "When are you going to quit trying to change me?" Again she pulled away from his touch. "Why should I run home and wring my hands? What good will that do? Maybe I can think of a way to really help! Give me some time to think."

"I'm leaving tomorrow afternoon." His voice was flat and cold. "I hope you'll join me. Your parents need *you*—not your dreams."

Temple tried to keep her voice even. "Call me in the morning."

She heard him leave the apartment, but she kept her gaze on the street below. Tears welled in her eyes and streamed down her cheeks. What am I going to do? What *can* I do?

Temple entered the club and smiled at the bartender. "Is Viv here?"

"Right here." Vivian stood up from behind the bar. She placed a clipboard on the bartop and smiled at Temple. "Glad you came in early, Temple. I've got to talk to you about something."

"Actually, that's why I'm here early. I've got something to discuss with you."

Vivian motioned toward her office. "Let's go in here, shall we?"

Temple followed her inside the small, cramped office. A large desk took up most of the available space. Temple sat in a straight-backed chair and waited for Viv to settle in the chair behind the desk.

"Me first." Vivian placed a pair of glasses on her nose. "This is business. Temple, do you belong to the union?"

"The union?"

Vivian sighed. "I thought as much. It never occurred to me until today when I was reading your employment information." She picked up a sheet of paper and let her gaze roam over it for a moment. "Under 'Affiliations' you didn't put anything down."

Temple nodded. "Right. Am I supposed to be a member?"

Viv took the glasses off and placed them on the desk. Her face was somber. "I'm afraid so, honey. If you're not a member, I can't hire you."

The news was too much for Temple's frayed nerves. With a trembling sob, she let the tears flow. She buried her face in her hands and felt Vivian's arms enfold her.

"Honey, it's not the end of the world. All you

have to do is apply for membership and pay your dues. Within a week or two I'll be able to hire you back." Vivian stroked Temple's hair. "There, there. Pull yourself together."

"It's not j-just that." Temple sucked in some air and tried to steady her voice. "Everything's gone wrong."

"What are you talking about? Wait here; I'll get you a drink and you can tell me all about it."

Temple waited for Vivian to return. She dried her eyes and tried to halt the shuddering sobs that still shook her body.

"Here, drink this." Vivian handed her the glass. "Slow. It's strong."

Temple nodded and tasted the drink. It burned her throat, spreading a heady warmth through her body. She took a deep breath and told Vivian about Jeremy's visit. Vivian listened, shaking her head.

"That's a tough problem, honey. I really don't have any snap solution." She squeezed Temple's hand. "You go back home and relax. Let me talk to a few people about this. Maybe they'll have some answers. Okay?"

"Okay." Temple finished the drink and felt a little stronger. "I shouldn't expect miracles, I guess. Jeremy's right. I should face facts."

Vivian smiled and led her to the door. "Hold on to those dreams, Temple. You'll be surprised how often they help get you through the bad times in life. I'll call you tomorrow and let you know if I've found any miracle workers."

"Thanks, Viv." On impulse Temple hugged

the other woman. She felt the tears prick her eyes again and she hurried away.

The sun leaked through the wooden window shutters. Bright shafts of light fell through the slats and spilled onto the floor at Temple's feet.

She edged the toe of one house slipper toward a band of sunlight and fet the warmth penetrate the satin material. She wiggled her toe, then drew her foot back. She reached for her coffee cup and stared at the telephone, willing it to ring.

Come on, Viv, she pleaded silently. Please call me before Jeremy calls and wants my decision!

The telephone remained obstinately silent, and Temple sighed. She stretched and looked at the clock again. Seven o'clock. No wonder I feel like I have lead weights on my eyes, she thought. I've been up since three this morning. She could feel the ache in her joints when she stretched and the dull throb resting behind her forehead.

No use trying to sleep until I find out my fate, she thought with a frown. The thought of going back with Jeremy made the coffee taste bitter in her mouth. She made a face and put the cup on the table.

Jeremy. How sensible he is—and that's what he wants me to be, too. Sensible. He always wears a sensible pin-stripe suit and a sensible tie. I'll bet even his pajamas are sensible. She shook her head.

She told herself she shouldn't be so mean. After all, Jeremy was trying to help her parents and even now was only looking out for their best interests. He was really very sweet.

And he'll convince me to marry him within two months if I go back to New York, she added. Yes. The pressure would build again. Before she knew it, she'd be planning a wedding, a wedding she was absolutely certain she didn't want. She might be crazy for reacting so strongly to Zack, but at least the strength of those reactions had proved to her that she would be even crazier to consider marrying Jeremy.

Marriage to Jeremy. She closed her eyes and imagined herself sitting on the sofa with Jeremy beside her. He'd be telling her about his day. A typical boring day at the office. She'd tell him about her day. Boring, too. They would plan to do something really different over the weekend. They would go see a movie.

"No!" Temple covered her face with her hands to block out the image and blurted the word aloud. Then what sounded like a knock on the door penetrated her mind, and she dropped her hands from her face to listen.

Yes. Someone was at the door. She shivered. It was Jeremy; she was sure of it. He must have decided to come for her answer in person. She gathered her courage and moved slowly toward the door, knowing that as soon as she opened it she would have to give up her dreams, probably forever.

The knocking came again, and this time the sound was so impatient that Temple almost ran the last few steps to the door. She opened it with her eyes downcast, unwilling to meet Jeremy's.

As she slowly raised them they encountered a strong brown throat above an open-necked shirt that revealed a chest sprinkled with curly black hair. *Not Jeremy,* she thought, and then gulped as she realized who stood before her.

"Hello, Zack. I haven't seen you in a while."

He smiled. "I've come to offer you a miracle. Why don't you ask me in?"

She stumbled a little as he shouldered past her without waiting for an invitation. By the time she'd closed the door and walked back into the living room, he was already settled comfortably on the sofa, lighting a cigarette. She waited for him to speak.

"I've talked to Viv about your . . . problem."

Temple sat on the edge of the armchair. She clenched her teeth and waited.

He watched her through dark eyes for a few seconds before he continued. "I'm very sorry to hear about your parents. However, I'm sure something can be worked out. Have you ever heard of a dowry?"

"Yes. Of course."

"Well, I propose that we turn the tables. The followers of Women's Liberation would applaud my offer. I suggest that I offer *you* a dowry in return for your hand in marriage."

Temple felt her heart stop, then start pumping again in a frenzy. "Marriage? To you?" Her voice almost broke on the last word and she wondered how she could speak at all.

A lazy smile, much like the one he'd worn the first time she'd seen him, graced his mouth.

How can he appear so nonchalant? she wondered. How can he keep his voice so low and steady?

"Yes, marriage. In return, I'd be happy to pay your father's debts. I understand how tricky these business deals can be. Your father gambled and lost."

"A crook stole his money!" Temple felt that she needed to defend her father. He wasn't a gambler!

Zack nodded. "Yes. He must have seen your father coming." He put his cigarette out in an ashtray. "There's a chance that the authorities might apprehend the man, of course, and your father might get some of the money back—but probably not all of it. The same thing happened to my brother a few years ago. He recovered a few hundred dollars, but he lost several thousand more." Zack glanced around the room. "Could I have a cup of coffee?"

Temple nodded and went to the kitchen. Her hands were trembling as she poured the black coffee into the cup, set it on a tray with milk and sugar, and returned to the living room.

"Ah, thank you." He waved away the milk and sugar. "In any case, I'd like it very much if you'd marry me."

Temple knew it was her turn to talk, but her throat felt dry and the throbbing in her head had increased. She rubbed at her temples and tried to think about his proposition.

"Why are you offering me this? What do you get out of it? I know you don't love me."

He sipped at the hot coffee for a moment. "I think we might grow to be . . . fond of each other. However, I would be willing to sign a contract stating that, after a year, if one or both of us want out of the marriage, we'll be free to obtain a divorce. That's fair, isn't it?"

Temple stood and paced the room for a few moments, trying to make sense of this totally unexpected development. Finally, she faced him.

"But, what do you get out of it?"

"A wife, and a few people off my back." He placed the coffee cup back on the tray and leaned forward, resting his elbows on his knees. "I'm a very eligible bachelor, Temple. Certain members of my family and a few well-meaning friends are eager to see me marry again, and some of them are pushing me to marry one woman in particular." He shrugged his wide shoulders. "I'm not interested in her. I *am* interested in you. I think that a marriage between us would be a very good thing—for both of us."

"But I don't know anything about you!" She looked at the man across from her. A man who wanted to be her husband. A stranger.

Again he gave her that lazy smile. He leaned back against the soft cushions and sighed. "I'm wealthy. I own a lot property and a cruise line. I have a large home on this island, where my mother lives. My brother and his wife live on the adjoining property. I was married to Giselle. She's dead. There. Satisfied?"

The question kept nagging at the corners of

Temple's mind and she voiced it. "What about—Candice?"

His smile became more forced and his eyes darkened. "Candice? What about her?"

"How will she take this . . . marriage? Isn't she the woman people are pushing in your direction?" Temple refused to back down, even though she saw his jaw tense again.

"I wouldn't waste time worrying about Candice if I were you." The ebony gaze flitted over Temple's face. "She won't be broken-hearted; believe me, she's not the type."

Temple examined his closed expression. Not the type? His answer bothered her, but she shrugged the uneasy feeling away and ticked off her next question. "Where would we live?"

He seemed relieved at the change of topic. "At my home here. You like the island?"

"Oh, yes!" Temple sat in one of the chairs. "I love this island. I don't want to go home at all, but I suppose I should."

"You don't have to go back to the States if you don't want to. What would that accomplish? Your father need never know the basis for our marriage."

"Oh, no! I would never want my parents to know why I married you!" She stared at him and watched the smile tug at the corner of his mouth.

"Is that a yes to my offer?"

Temple blinked. "I—I don't know." She closed her eyes, blotting out his face. A thousand questions seemed to ricochet around in her head.

Could she marry this man, just like that? Heaven knows, she was halfway to being in love with him already! But marriage? What if she was miserable? What if a year seemed too long to stay with him? What if I fall *all* the way in love with him? she asked herself.

"I just wanted to make it on my own." At first she wasn't sure if she'd even voiced her thought.

"Independence is a frame of mind, Temple."

She opened her eyes and found him looking at her. Was he right? she wondered.

"I—I couldn't work at the club, could I?"

A frown creased his brow. "I don't think that would be proper. Besides, you'll be married to a well-known man. People here know me. They'd wonder why my wife was employed at a club. A club I own."

"Yes. Yes, of course." Temple wondered why his answer didn't bother her. Confused, she rested against the chair cushions and allowed the thoughts crowding her mind free rein. She mulled over each question, ignoring the man who sat a few feet from her.

The rapping at the door propelled her from the chair. She glanced at Zack before she went to answer. Her heart climbed into her throat when she saw Jeremy standing in the hall.

"Jeremy! I thought you were going to call!" She stood aside to let him enter the apartment. He stopped just inside the door, his eyes fastened on Zack.

Temple saw the suspicion glint in his eyes when he looked at Zack's unbuttoned shirt and then at the casual caftan and slippers she was wearing. She felt anger engulf her at his implied question and lifted her chin.

"Jeremy, this is Zachary St. James. Zachary, Jeremy Carlton."

Zack rose slowly from the sofa and extended his hand. "A pleasure, Jeremy. Temple's told me all about you."

Temple flashed Zachary a biting glance. Told him about Jeremy! she fumed inwardly. I've never even mentioned him! Vivian. The name whipped through her mind. Yes. Vivian must have told him.

"Nice to meet you." Jeremy's voice was cold. "I suppose Temple has told you that she's leaving St. Thomas."

Zack sat down again. He rested his head against one hand, his arm propped along the sofa back. His dark gaze swept Temple's flushed face. "She's told me about her father's misfortune, yes."

Jeremy cleared his throat. "Yes. Well, she's needed at home."

Cold fury raced through Temple. She glared at Jeremy's back. "Will you stop talking about me as if I'm not even in the room!"

He whirled to face her, and she was struck by the contrast between the two men. Jeremy seemed so boyish next to Zachary's moody good looks. She remembered how much taller Zachary seemed than Jeremy, yet surely only a few inches were in Zack's favor. It was the way he held himself. So tall. So erect. So powerful.

"You *are* leaving."

Temple held herself rigid, trying to keep her

temper in check. "I said I would give you my decision this morning. I don't recall agreeing to anything."

"Well, yes. But I assumed you'd. make the sensible choice."

Temple felt ready to scream. "Sensible! Sensible! Why is it that your way is always the most sensible?" She threw the word at him. He flinched, but she continued. "I won't be forced into doing something I don't want to do just because you think it's right! I'm a grown woman and I make my own decisions!"

She paused and took two or three gulping breaths. Jeremy's face seemed to be carved of stone; only his eyes seemed to have any life in them.

"Okay," he said levelly. "What is your decision?"

Temple looked at Zachary now. A gentle smile curved his mouth, and his eyes seemed softer now than before. His whole attitude seemed supportive. She turned to focus on Jeremy. That cold mask still covered his face, yet, beneath that, she could see something else. Confidence?

She squared her shoulders, stiffened her back, and faced Jeremy. "Zack is going to give my father the money he needs as a—a—wedding present to me."

"What?" Jeremy gripped her upper arms. "Are you crazy? What wedding? You can't be serious."

Temple flinched at the pain as his fingers dug into her flesh. "I'm quite serious. I'm going to marry Zack."

Jeremy released her and turned to Zack. "Is that true?"

Before Zack could speak, Temple grabbed Jeremy's arm. "Why are you asking him? I just told you that it's true! I'm going to marry him."

Jeremy ran a hand through his hair. His eyes seemed to burn into Temple. "I can't believe this. I—I need a drink."

Temple sighed and looked at Zack. "Zack, could you leave us alone for a while, please?"

He stood. "Of course. I'll call you in an hour or so." He paused near the door. "Don't worry, Jeremy. I'll take good care of her."

"Tell me this is a joke," Jeremy said as soon as the door had closed behind Zack.

Temple poured some brandy into a glass and handed it to him. She almost felt sorry for him when she saw the deep lines at the corners of his mouth.

"It's not a joke, Jeremy. I'm going to marry him."

"Why?" He downed the drink quickly.

Temple tried to laugh. "For the obvious reasons."

A sneer curled his upper lip, and he set the glass down on the table. "Don't give me that! You coudn't possibly be in love with him, or you would have told me yesterday!" His face looked drained of color. "Don't you realize that you're as bad as a prostitute? You're selling yourself, and don't try to kid yourself that it's anything else."

"Shut up!" Temple's hand flew hard against his cheek, and she watched as the skin was flooded with bright color. She placed her hand to her mouth, shocked at her own action. "Jeremy—I—"

He shook his head and headed for the door. "You'll regret this, Temple." He turned back to face her. "Just remember, when it gets too awful, you have only yourself to blame."

Chapter Five

Temple rested her head against the chair and closed her eyes. She listened to the hum of the plane's engines and felt the throbbing pulse beneath her. Fatigue seemed to envelop her and she relaxed, allowing her tense muscles and frayed nerves to rest. She turned away from the window, with its view of the ocean below, and closed her eyes, letting her surroundings slip away.

She thought about her destination, and about all the things that had so suddenly changed in her life. She would be in St. Thomas again, but not as Temple Anderson this time. Now she was Temple St. James. The name sounded ominous, and she shivered.

She had never even seen the house that was now to be her home. What would it look like? Would it be massive—like a castle, perhaps? Maybe it would be a modest home. A modern home, even. And what of the people who already lived there? Would they accept her as easily as her parents had accepted Zack?

A rueful smile curved her lips. How quickly Zack had won her parents' hearts and trust. She had decided to go back to New York to see them after all, and after the initial uncomfortable introductions and puzzlement, Zack had caught them up in his spell.

Temple recalled the lengthy discussions he'd held with her father. For hours the two men had talked of nothing but business and investments. Zack had told her father about what had happened to his brother. What was his brother's name? She searched her memory. Samson, that was it. And Samson was married to . . . Laura. Temple remembered how quickly her father had warmed to Zack. Hesitant at first to accept Zack's money, within a few hours her father was calling Zack "son." And her mother! Temple sighed. Zack had only had to compliment her mother a few times and give her that disarming smile. What a pushover! Like me, Temple thought. Just like me. I fell for those charms quickly enough, too.

Oh, but how happy they had looked at the wedding. Her father, so proud, so pleased. Her mother, looking years younger and shedding a few token tears. Yes, they were happy now, Temple thought.

She recalled how her mother had embraced her after the wedding ceremony and whispered in her ear, "Temple, darling, you've married such a fine man. I'm so very happy for you."

Have I? Temple wondered. Have I married a fine man? She lifted her lashes a fraction and peered at the man seated next to her. Her husband. Those dark, searching eyes moved quickly over the magazine in front of him, taking everything in. He wore the same dark suit he had been married in, and a red rose still rested on his lapel.

Temple let her lashes brush her cheek, shutting out his image. Why can't I shake this feeling of dread? Of shame? she asked herself. Is it true? Am I no better than a prostitute? A gold digger? She could hear Jeremy's accusations still. Had he been right?

Zachary had upheld his part of the bargain, and now it was her turn to pay the piper. What would that payment be? She shuddered. Why hadn't she forced him to be more specific about what would be expected of her before she signed that contract? She'd committed herself to a man she hardly even knew and she didn't have the slightest idea of what would be expected of her.

Her parents' faces appeared behind her eyelids. She saw again the look of relief on her father's face, the expression of love in her mother's eyes.

Yes, she told herself. It was worth it. No matter what she had to go through, it was worth it to have brought such happiness to the people who loved her most in all the world. They had always tried, perhaps too hard at times, to take care of her; now it was her turn to take care of them.

"Why are you frowning, Temple?" Zack's voice seemed to come from very far away.

She lifted her lashes but didn't meet his eyes, though she could feel them on her.

"Was I?"

"Yes."

"I was trying to remember your mother's name," she lied.

"Her name is Suzanne."

"And what shall I call her?"

"Whatever you feel like calling her, I suppose."

"I'll call her Mrs. St. James."

"*You're* Mrs. St. James. Mother remarried; she's now Mrs. Cifford Stevens."

She looked at him, taking in his stern expression and the business magazine now resting on his lap. "You didn't tell me that she was remarried."

"Yes, I did. Just now." His eyes mocked her. "Clifford lives at the house, too."

"Your father . . . he's dead?"

"Yes; he died when I was fifteen. He sold real estate."

"Did he own the cruise line?"

He smiled and shook his head. "No. I purchased the cruise line ten years ago. At the moment we have three ships and we're working on another. She sails in a few weeks."

"What does your stepfather do?"

"Nothing; he's retired." Zachary signaled for the stewardess, who came quickly to his side. He handed her the magazine and ordered a drink. "What do you want to drink, Temple?"

"Just orange juice, please."

He shrugged. "Very well. Aren't you feeling well?"

Temple watched the stewardess move away to the galley. "Not really. The past few days have been rather hectic, and I think it's catching up with me."

"Once we're home you'll have plenty of time to rest. You'll enjoy Saint's Summit."

"Saint's Summit?"

"Yes. That's the name of my—our—home."

Temple averted her eyes and tried to ignore the soft caress in his voice. She suddenly remembered the night when he had told her that he wanted her, meant to have her. "I take it that the house is on a hill?" she asked, forcing her thoughts back to the conversation at hand.

"Yes. On the crest of a hill, overlooking the sea. It's quite lovely."

"What did you tell your family about me?"

"That I had married you."

"Didn't they wonder about it? I mean, it was all so sudden."

He shook his head and took his drink from the stewardess, who then handed Temple her orange juice. "They were too happy that I'd married at all to spend a lot of time wondering why. I'm sure they assumed we had the usual motives." He smiled mockingly, though it seemed to Temple that his mockery was directed as much against himself as against her.

Temple sipped the tangy juice. "I hope they like me."

"They will. You can be quite charming when you put your mind to it."

She glanced at him and saw the teasing glint

in his eyes. He reached for her hand and studied the ruby and diamond wedding band. "That looks nice. We have excellent taste."

Temple tried to smile. Her gaze moved from her fingers to his, and the gold and silver wedding band resting around his third finger.

She pulled her hand from his. Married. The word seemed to stick in her mind like a thorn. I'm a bride and I'm on my honeymoon. She repeated the sentence in her mind, but the words seemed to hold no truth.

Temple leaned forward and peered past Andrew's shoulder. The large electronic gate was opening slowly, and she saw the large *S* woven into the intricate ironwork of the gate. The car eased forward and continued along the winding private road.

On either side Temple could see lush foliage. Unspoiled land, she thought with relief. No tennis courts or manicured gardens, just tall trees and wild flowers.

"There." Zack's hand rested on her shoulder as he spoke. "There's the house."

Temple sucked in her breath at the sight of the house, which came into view as they rounded a final curve. There, at the top of a sheer cliff, stood a two-story house of pink sandstone with sunlight reflecting on the large windows and the red-shingled roof.

"It looks like pink sugar," Temple whispered.

"Yes. Do you like it?"

She nodded and let her eyes roam over the arched roof and the baskets of green plants suspended from the porch ceiling. At one end of the porch she could even see a white swing.

Andrew braked to a stop in front of the house. Temple looked to her left and saw the green lawn that stopped abruptly at the cliff's edge. Below, the sea glistened in the summer sun.

She stepped from the car, and Zack wrapped his arm around her waist when he followed to stand by her side. She started to nudge him away but stopped when a white-haired woman appeared in the doorway.

"Zack!" She ran down the steps and planted a kiss on his cheek. Her eyes moved to Temple. "Temple? I'm Zack's mother." She kissed Temple, then stood back. "Welcome to Saint's Summit."

"Are they finally here?"

Temple looked past the woman to the man who had spoken and now stood on the porch. His bald head reflected the sun, and his smile was bright.

"Clifford, this is Temple!" Zack's mother grabbed Temple's hand and pulled her toward the older man.

"Zack, what a beauty!" Clifford shook Temple's hand, then slapped Zack on the back. "A beauty!"

"I agree." Zack flashed her a smile. "Come on in, Temple; take a look at your home."

A shiver of excitement shot through Temple as she climbed the steps and walked toward the front door. In one fluid motion a strong arm slipped beneath her knees and she felt her feet leave the ground. A gasp caught in her throat and she automatically wound her arms about Zack's neck. Her eyes sought his, and she caught the glint of humor in the dark depths. His mouth, close to her cheek, twisted in a wry smile.

"I believe this is the custom, isn't it?" His voice was low and husky, sending a new shiver through her.

Cool shadows enveloped them as Zack carried her over the threshold and into the foyer. She caught sight of the pink, gray, and white marble staircase before Zack swung her to her feet. Temple let her arms slip from his neck and felt hot color stain her cheeks at the intimate look Zack gave her. She averted her eyes and saw that the same tricolor marble was beneath her feet.

"Daddy! Daddy! He's here! He's here!"

The high-pitched words echoed through the foyer, and Temple raised her head in shock to encounter a blond, blue-eyed little girl bounding down the stairs. Arms outstretched, the child ran toward Zack. A bright smile deepened the dimples in her round, flushed cheeks.

Zack bent and scooped the child up in his arms. He planted a kiss on her puckered mouth and hugged her, while she peered shyly at Temple.

Temple felt the color drain from her face. She could hardly believe the evidence of her eyes and ears. Zachary had a child! She stared at the lovely little girl who nestled her cheek against his. Had this been his real reason for marrying her? she wondered. To raise his child? To raise

Giselle's child? She had been such a fool. Half in love with him, and worried about her parents, she had been too caught up in her own problems to wonder very long about his reasons for wanting this marriage. What a fool she had been not to have questioned him further, but she had never expected anything like this.

Zack's dark eyes found hers, and she knew that he noticed her pale face and accusing eyes. A frown touched his mouth and the muscles in his jaw flexed.

A movement on the stairs drew Temple's gaze from the stern expression that rested on Zack's face to the top of the stairs, where a dark-haired man in white trousers and a pale blue shirt stood looking down at the scene in the hall.

"Ah! The bride and groom make their entrance at last!" The man's voice preceded him down the stairs.

"Daddy! Look! It's Uncle Zack!" The child hugged Zack again and giggled.

Uncle Zack! Temple sought Zack's eyes again and saw the hard, angry glint there. Feeling like a complete fool, she turned toward the man.

"Hello. I'm Samson, your brother-in-law." He grasped her hand, then looked at his brother. "Zack, you have excellent taste."

"Yes, don't I?" Zack's voice was guarded. "Molly, this is your Aunt Temple."

Wide blue eyes focused on Temple before a curtain of blond lashes fell to conceal them. "Hullo," she said in a tiny voice.

Temple touched the child's dimpled elbow. "Hello, Molly. It's very nice to meet you."

91

"Molly has contracted a sudden shyness, it seems," Samson said, taking his daughter from Zack's arms. "You're going to like this lady, Molly. She's your new aunt. Don't you think she's pretty?"

Molly examined Temple for a moment, then murmured, "Yes. She's got pretty hair—like Uncle Zack's."

Samson laughed. "Molly has a thing for dark hair. Like mine, too, huh, Molly?"

Molly's small fingers curled into the black hair at her father's neck and she giggled. "Uh-huh. Like yours, too. I wish I had pretty hair."

"But your hair is lovely, Molly." Temple stroked the fair curls that covered the youngster's head. "Your hair looks like sunlight."

"Like sunlight?" The blue eyes grew larger. "Really?"

Temple nodded. "Really."

"So! The master returns to the manor and he brings the mistress with him!"

Temple turned to see a tall blond woman walking toward her. Molly's mother, she thought, as she took in the blue eyes and dimpled cheeks.

"You must be Laura," Temple said, extending her hand.

As the woman's hand closed over hers Temple noticed her long fingers and the nails that were painted blood red.

"Yes. And you're Temple"—Laura glanced at Zack for confirmation—"Zack's new wife." Temple could read nothing in her tone.

Zack's mother had come in behind them. "Now that the introductions have been made," she said, "let's go out to the sun porch for some refreshments. Temple, Zack, if you'd like to freshen up first, we'll wait for you before we pour tea."

Zack nodded and touched Temple's elbow. "That sounds fine. I'll just show Temple our room, and then we'll join you."

He propelled Temple toward the staircase, and she felt a definite sense of relief at getting away from all the new faces. She hadn't expected to meet quite so many people on her first day back. Had she been what they expected?

Her eyes were drawn to the wallpaper in the hallway. It was printed with flowered vines, making the hallway seem almost like a garden pathway. Zack stopped at the end of the hall. Through the arch Temple could see a set of dark wood double doors.

"These are our apartments." Zack opened the doors and stepped back to let Temple enter ahead of him.

A queen-size bed was the most noticeable feature of the room. A white mosquito net was draped from ceiling to floor around the bed, and Temple could see a gold and brown satin bedspread through the thin netting. Several white chests of drawers with attached mirrors and white wicker furniture completed the furnishings, while the drapes were brown and gold satin to match the spread. The room seemed flooded with sunlight, and Temple lifted her eyes to the ceiling. A soft gasp filtered through her parted lips when she saw the skylight directly over the bed.

Zack brushed past her, but she stood rooted to the spot, burying her feet deeper in the plush white carpet. Luxury seemed to engulf her.

"Here is the dressing area, and beyond that is the bathroom." He motioned to an archway. "Is it all too much for you, songbird?"

She spun toward him, surprised at his use of the pet name.

"That *is* what Scrappy calls you, isn't it?"

"Y-yes, but . . ."

"I like it; it suits you."

The sudden intimacy of the atmosphere brought butterflies to Temple's stomach. She glanced around the room, as if looking for a means of escape.

Zack crossed the room and stood squarely in front of her. "How do you like your new home?"

"It's beautiful, and your family seems wonderful, too. I hope they like me."

"They do. Besides, now they're *your* family, too."

"Y-yes." Temple forced a laugh. "I suppose they are, at that." She looked at her tightly clasped fingers. "Well, shall we . . .?" Her voice trailed off when she felt Zack's fingertip touch her chin. With insistent pressure he forced her chin up.

"Look at me, Temple." The command came huskily through his lips. "Look at me!"

Slowly she lifted her lashes. Her heart

thumped painfully against her rib cage when she saw the smoldering passion in his eyes.

"I know that all of this is strange to you, and I know that you got quite a shock when you assumed that Molly was my child. Did you really think that I would marry you without telling you I had a child?"

"I—I didn't know what to think." Temple couldn't force her voice above a whisper.

"Yes, well, we both have a lot to learn about each other. Take your time; I won't rush you." His eyes darkened again and came to rest on her lips.

Temple shivered as she watched his face blur before her. A hot current of emotion seared through her when his lips brushed hers. His hand left her chin, and she felt his fingers at the nape of her neck. His lips touched hers again, seeming to melt against them, forcing hers to part. His kiss was a claim of total possession, and she felt lost as his arms locked her body against his. The firm pressure of his mouth and body swept away her last vestige of defense, and Temple rested limply against him.

Gently his lips left hers, and his hands curved around her shoulders to hold her away from him. Liquid fire stirred in his eyes as he looked at her, and Temple felt weak and helpless in the face of his magnetic gaze.

"Perhaps we should join the others before we lose ourselves completely?"

She nodded and tried to straighten in his hold. He draped an arm around her shoulders to lead her from the room. Temple felt almost light-hearted for the first time since she had decided to enter into this strange marriage when she looked at his face and saw the smile there.

"I know you're tired, but let's have tea and then you can rest. Okay?"

Again she nodded, but she couldn't tear her eyes away from that smile. That smile is just for me, she thought, and her heart soared with the knowledge.

Temple eyed the rattan furniture, pastel-colored cushions, and lush plants that filled the sitting room. Nestled in the deep cushions of the sofa, she enjoyed the tropical feel of the room. Outside, she knew, the air held the tangy scent of exotic blossoms, and the sea was crashing in salty waves against the cliff. Everything was still new to her, and even after several hours of conversation and a dinner with Zack's family she felt unsure. And as the sky darkened she felt the stirrings of a new apprehension. What would Zack expect of her tonight?

"Would you like more wine, Temple?"

She jumped in her chair before turning to Zack. "Yes, thank you."

She watched him cross to the bar. The navy-blue trousers seemed to accent his powerful thighs, and the white open-necked heavy silk shirt only served to emphasize the deep tan of his skin. She watched the play of muscles beneath his shirt as he poured the pale liquid into the glasses.

"Have you checked out the progress on *The*

Mermaid?" Zack's deep voice was directed at Samson.

"Yes; we're right on schedule. She'll sail on time."

"Did those wall murals add the right effect?"

"Yes; they're fabulous. Especially the one in the dining room."

Zack recrossed the room and handed one newly filled wine goblet to Temple. "Mother, you're still planning on being my representative on *The Mermaid*'s maiden voyage, aren't you?"

Mrs. Stevens glanced at her husband. "Clifford and I assumed that you'd probably changed your mind, that you'd want to take Temple on that cruise."

Zack smiled at Temple. "Oh, I'd much rather take Temple on a private cruise aboard *Saint's Escape.*"

Temple felt a fan of pink cover her face at the idea of a private cruise with Zack. "What's *Saint's Escape?*"

"My yacht."

"Of course!" Mrs. Stevens beamed. "That's a much better idea."

Temple thought again of herself alone on a private yacht with Zack, and her nerves tingled. There would be no interruptions there. No chance of escape from his overpowering presence. A question slipped into her mind. Why was she always searching for an escape from him? After all, she thought, he was her husband. But he didn't love her, and that was what she was running from—a loveless relationship. She resolutely ignored the small voice that urged her to define her own feelings for Zack. That way, she was sure, lay only confusion and pain.

"I hope you'll like *Saint's Escape* more than Giselle did," Laura said. "Zack, remember how she hated it? She said it was your escape from her."

Temple's blood ran cold when she saw Zack's suddenly hooded gaze. His eyes were like chips of ebony when he looked at Laura.

"Yes. I remember." His voice sent a chill up Temple's spine, and it was apparent that she hadn't been the only one to feel its effect.

"Listen, it's time we headed home," Samson said, breaking the silence. "Come on, Laura. I'll go get Molly."

"She's in the Green Room," Mrs. Stevens said. "I checked on her a few minutes ago and she was sound asleep."

Temple watched Samson leave the room. He looks like Zachary, she thought, but he isn't as tall or as powerfully built. And his eyes are only gray, not a brown that can deepen to midnight black.

"I'll help you get your things," Mrs. Stevens said, placing an arm about Laura's shoulders and urging her to the door.

Laura offered Zack a tight smile. "Nice to have you back, Zachary." Her blue eyes found Temple, and her voice was perceptibly cooler as she said, "Welcome to Saint's Summit, Temple. I'm sure I'll be seeing you."

"Thank you, Laura."

Laura turned to Zack again. "Sorry if I upset you, Zachary."

Zack arched his eyebrows and one corner of his mouth lifted. "You didn't upset me, Laura. It takes more than *that* to upset me."

Bright color spotted Laura's cheeks, and she turned and hurried from the room. Mrs. Stevens looked worriedly at Zack before she followed her daughter-in-law from the room.

Clifford cleared his throat and tossed Zack a sheepish grin. "Laura doesn't mean anything, Zack. It's just that she and Giselle were so close."

"I know." Zachary drained his wineglass and crossed the room to stand by the floor-to-ceiling windows, turning his back to the room.

Temple shifted uneasily. Electric tension seemed to hang in the room. Had it been the mention of Giselle that had thrown such a sudden chill over things? She studied her husband's broad back. He seemed so aloof now, his mind somewhere else. Was he thinking of Giselle? Did he miss her?

Clifford rose from his seat at his wife's entrance. "Ready for our evening stroll, dear?"

"Yes. Just let me get my shawl," Mrs. Stevens replied before quickly leaving again.

Clifford turned to Zack. "Zack, would you and Temple like to join us? It's a lovely evening."

Zack looked over his shoulder. "What?" His brows met. "Oh, no thanks." He turned back to the window. "You go ahead, Temple."

Clifford held out a hand to her. "Please join us."

Temple looked over to Zachary, who seemed completely unaware of her. Quickly making up her mind, she followed Clifford to the foyer, where Mrs. Stevens waited for them.

"Are you coming, Temple? It will be nice to have you along." She looked at Temple's sleeveless sundress. "Should you take a wrap?"

"Oh, no, I'll be fine."

Temple followed the couple out of the house. Floodlights were set among the bushes scattered across the lawn, lending light to the dark night. She could hear the pounding of the surf against the massive rocks, and when she looked up she saw gray whiffs of cloud floating between the earth and the stars.

"Lovely night, isn't it?" Clifford asked.

"Oh, yes." Temple breathed in the night air.

"We take a stroll every evening before we turn in," Mrs. Stevens said.

"Mrs. Stevens . . ." Temple stopped as she noticed the frown on the other woman's face.

"Let's not be so formal. Won't you call me Suzanne?"

"Of course—if you really want me to."

"I insist," the older woman said, squeezing Temple's arm. "Now, what were you about to say?"

"Does Zachary ever join you on your walk?"

"No. He usually takes this time to do some paperwork, keep up with last-minute changes and developments, you understand."

Temple's attention strayed to a shadowy structure in the distance. "What's that?"

"It's the summerhouse," Clifford answered.

Temple turned and looked back at the house. No wonder she hadn't noticed it when they'd arrived; several trees hid it from view. She looked back at the structure. Now that she was closer, she could make out the walls broken up by large windows and the tile roof.

Clifford led the way toward the small building and Temple stepped inside. Panes of stained glass were suspended from the ceiling, and she imagined how the sun would play on the glass, casting bright pools of color over the walls and floor. Lacy ferns and flowering bougainvillea grew in stone pots that rested in each corner of the building. Stone benches ran the length of each wall, and a three-tiered fountain in the center gurgled as water bubbled from the top and fell to the tiers below.

"I love it!" Temple clasped her hands together and turned to face Clifford and Suzanne. "It's enchanting! It must be twice as beautiful during the day."

"Yes, once the sun goes down a bit, that is. It can get quite hot in here during the heat of the day," Suzanne said. Suddenly Suzanne covered Temple's hands with her own and bestowed a bright smile on the younger woman. "I just want to tell you how very happy we are to have you in our family."

Temple felt a rush of warmth and she matched Suzanne's smile. "That's very kind of you."

"I second the sentiment," Clifford told her. "We're all pleased that Zachary has found someone like you."

"So many women are interested only in a man's bank account." A disgusted expression flitted across Suzanne's face as she spoke. "We were so afraid that Zachary might be trapped by a gold digger. Heaven knows he's kept company with a few who I was sure were only interested in his fortune. Now we can rest easy. It's obvious that you two love each other."

Temple felt a pang of guilt and she pulled her hands from Suzanne's. She felt like a cheat and a liar and she fished desperately for another topic of conversation.

She cleared her throat. "Who—who designed the summerhouse?" She sat down on one of the stone benches and tried to calm her nerves.

"Zack. He designed Saint's Summit, too."

Temple stared at her mother-in-law. "Zack? I had no idea!"

"He's a man of many talents, hmmm?" Clifford gave her a sly wink.

Temple laughed uncomfortably. Then Suzanne, apparently sensitive to her discomfort, smiled and said, "I would imagine that right now our man of many talents is impatiently waiting for us to return his bride to him."

Temple placed a cool hand to her hot cheek and felt her fingers tremble. Of course Zack was waiting for her. This was their wedding night.

As if in a dream, she followed the older couple back to the main house. With each step her nerves grew tauter. Now it was her turn to make good their bargain. Her knees trembled as she walked across the porch and into the foyer.

The house was quiet, and Temple wondered if Zack had already retired to their bedroom.

"Can you find your way, Temple?"

Temple turned to Zack's mother. "Yes."

"Well, goodnight. Clifford and I are just going to have a cup of tea in the sitting room before we call it a night."

Temple wanted to invite herself to join them, but she knew they would think it strange. Instead, she smiled and began mounting the stairs. She walked down the vine-papered hallway and stood beneath the arch. The doors were closed, and Temple placed a hand to her stomach and took two deep breaths before she opened them. She didn't see Zack, so she tiptoed in for a quick look around. She moved quietly toward the dressing room. The room was large enough to house a daybed, two huge closets and a dressing table. Temple eyed the daybed before she entered the bathroom. The sunken bathtub and double sinks were cut from white marble, while brown-tiled floors and a matching shower cubicle added dark splashes of color.

She quickly left the bathroom and walked to one of the closets. She opened the shuttered doors, gasped, and stepped back.

Hundreds of garments were arrayed in front of her. She reached out and her fingers played with the fabrics. Silk, satin, cotton, wool. The colors ranged from pastels to smoky grays and sultry blacks. She rested her hand on a panel and gasped again when the panel swung away to reveal shelves. Several dozen pairs of shoes, grouped by color, rested on the shelves.

Hastily Temple shut the closet doors. Were those clothes hers? If so, how and when had they gotten here? She ran to one of the dressers and opened the top drawer. Lacy bras and panties, neatly folded, filled it almost to overflowing. She shut it and opened the next one. Nightgowns.

She pushed the new, unfamiliar garments aside and found a peach-colored negligee of her own. She closed the door and quickly undressed, taking the nightie with her into the bathroom. The shower looked inviting, and soon warm water caressed her skin while she relaxed and let weariness steal over her.

I'm so tired, she thought. I feel like I've lived six months during the last week. Reluctantly, she turned off the water and toweled herself dry. Then she dropped the soft folds of the negligee over her and walked into the bedroom.

She stumbled a bit in confusion when she saw Zachary, sitting in one of the wicker chairs by the windows. His dark gaze slid from her bare feet up the length of her body to her face.

"Didn't you find your new negligees?"

"Y-yes. I wasn't sure if they were mine."

His eyebrows rose. "Whose would they be, if not yours?"

"I don't know. Giselle's?"

His lids dropped to hood smoldering eyes. "That is a ridiculous assumption."

Temple began to tremble, and her stomach churned. She rubbed her damp palms on the thin fabric of her nightgown. When Zack rose from the chair her heart climbed into her throat and began to beat at a sickening tempo.

Her trembling increased as Zack strode toward her. He caught her shoulders in his strong grip.

"You're shaking. Are you cold? Scared? Or both?"

She swallowed and shrugged. His hold tightened.

"You should see yourself, songbird," he whispered. "Those blue eyes of yours are as large as half dollars. You look like a frightened little waif. Why are you scared of me?" He bent his head and touched his lips to the side of her neck. "I've bought you new clothes; I've brought you to a beautiful home. I've married you, Temple. Have I been anything but good to you?"

Temple stiffened. He *had* been good to her, maybe too good. But he had bought her, and she was just another possession among many, to be treated with the utmost care because she was expensive.

Temple looked at the bed and saw that the covers were turned down. Ready for her. She shivered.

Zachary lifted his head and studied her. She couldn't bear his gaze and moved away from him to sit on the bed. He gave her a questioning look.

"What's wrong?"

"Nothing." Her voice sounded strained, even to her own ears. "Let's not waste any time. I'm ready to fulfill my part of the bargain."

Anger glinted in his eyes, and he set his jaw in an unrelenting line. "You don't sound too thrilled with the prospect."

Temple shrugged, feigning indifference. "I'm not backing out. I'm certainly willing to give you what you paid for."

"How thoughtful of you." His voice was like sandpaper, scratching on Temple's already frayed nerve ends. "Why are you acting like this? What's gotten into you? Just a few weeks ago I thought you wanted this as much as I did. What's happened to suddenly change your mind?"

The anger that had been directed at herself spilled over and Temple heard her voice rise with sudden rage. "You've bought me a complete wardrobe and you've given me jewels." She held up her left hand so that her wedding band flashed. "What more can I ask for? You've paid me well, and now I'm perfectly willing to complete my part of the bargain. But don't flatter yourself that I did this for you, or because I was dying to throw myself into your arms. I did this for my parents, and you'll get what you paid for, but don't expect enthusiasm, too."

He took a few steps toward her, then stopped. His eyes were impossible to read. "I think I'd rather pay for my pleasures than take you in your present frame of mind."

Again the trembling jarred her body and Temple yearned to hurt him just as he was hurting her. "Isn't that what I am? Isn't that what you've made me? I'm just a high-class call girl!"

Her breath rasped in her throat when his hand reached out to tangle itself in her dark hair. He pulled her head back until her eyes met his.

"So that's how you feel? Like a call girl?" His

mouth thinned into a white, dangerous line. "You don't think much of yourself, do you?" He shrugged. "So why should I?"

A shaft of fear sliced through Temple as Zachary placed one knee on the bed beside her and bent to crush her lips with his own. She struggled to free herself from his bruising possession, but his fingers wrapped themselves more tightly in her hair and sent sharp pricks of pain through her scalp. He bruised her lips with the continued fury of his kiss.

Desperately she pushed at his shoulders, but he only lowered her onto the bed, his body pushing her down. She felt the heat of his hands through the thin fabric of her negligee as they roamed over the curves of her body. She tangled her fingers in his hair and pulled, finally freeing her mouth from his.

"Leave me alone!" Her voice cracked with fear.

A cruel smile twisted his mouth. "Why? Wasn't it you who said you were quite ready to fulfill our bargain?"

"No! Please, no!"

Her pleas were smothered by his hard mouth. He forced her lips apart so that his tongue could probe the soft inner recesses of her mouth, and one hard, muscled thigh pressed her into the depths of the mattress. She pounded at his shoulders and worked one leg free to kick against him.

His sharp intake of breath was music to her ears. He planted his hands on the pillows at either side of her head and directed his cold, angry words at her. "You fight dirty, Temple." His tone was pitched low, like a growl. "But don't worry." He lifted himself from her to stand beside the bed. "I'd much rather sleep alone than rest my head on your cold breast!"

Tears blurred her vision as she watched him stride toward the dressing room. The door slammed, and Temple closed her eyes. Weak from her struggle, and from fear, she turned her back to the dressing room and curled her body into a protective ball. Sobs racked her body and tears wet her hot cheeks. She sniffed and tried to stifle the sobs that rose in her throat. She gave up. Turning her head into the satin pillowcase she let misery consume her.

Chapter Six

An uncomfortable silence reigned over the breakfast room.

Temple looked across the table at Zack and reflected bitterly that, as always, he was the cause of it. He had been giving her the silent treatment for the past two weeks. Everyone sensed his anger, and no one knew quite how to react to it. Herself least of all, she thought unhappily.

She glanced at her mother-in-law and saw the strained lines that radiated from the corners of her mouth. She turned to Clifford, who gave her a weak smile.

Temple glared at Zachary. He seemed totally immune to the uncomfortable atmosphere. He held the morning paper in one hand and a cup of coffee in the other, reading the news as if nothing was the matter. She inspected his red V-necked sports shirt and crisp blue jeans. He's certainly dressed casually today, she thought. With a jolt, she realized it was Saturday. Maybe he wasn't going to work. If so, it would be the first day he'd taken off since their arrival—and the first chance she'd had to spend any time with him.

Temple pushed the eggs around on her plate with her fork and frowned. Had she been here only two weeks? It seemed like months.

She thought about the tense, angry atmosphere that dominated her bedroom. Every night Zachary waited until she had retired, then stalked to the dressing room to sleep on the daybed. Of course, she told herself, she was glad he wasn't sharing her bed, but he could be more discreet about it. Everyone must know they weren't sleeping together, and the fact that Zachary hadn't spoken a word to her in days didn't help matters.

She gave him a smoldering stare. He continued to read, totally immune to her anger. Her gaze moved to rest on his generous, firm mouth. A shiver raced along her spine as she recalled how cruel those lips could be—how hard and unyielding! But they could be soft and sensuous, too, she reminded herself. Those lips could spark a fire deep in her soul. . . .

"Hello, everybody!"

Temple glanced in the direction of the voice and forced herself to smile at Laura. They had met frequently during the last two weeks, and it had been obvious that Laura had no use for her.

"Laura!" Suzanne held out a welcoming hand to her daughter-in-law. "Where are Samson and Molly?"

"At home. They were sleepyheads this morning." She sat down and reached for a biscuit. "Could I have some coffee?"

"Of course." Clifford turned in his seat toward the swinging kitchen door. "Ophelia!"

A round, dimpled face peered around the door. "Yes, sir?"

"A cup of coffee for Mrs. St. James, please."

"Yes, sir." Ophelia smiled at Laura. "Good morning, Mrs. St. James."

"Morning, Ophelia." Laura smiled back at the woman, then glanced around the table. "We're awfully silent this morning. What's so interesting in the newspaper, Zachary?"

Zack turned the page, then looked at Laura over the top of the paper. "Lots of things. What are you going to do today?"

"We're going out on the boat. Fishing. You know how Molly loves to watch her daddy fish."

"You don't sound very excited about the idea."

"I'm not the fishing type, Zack. You know that." Laura shrugged. "I'll work on my tan."

Temple looked at Laura's ginger-brown arms and envied the tan she already had.

Ophelia bustled into the breakfast room and placed a cup of coffee before Laura. "Anything else, Mrs. St. James?"

"No, thanks, Ophelia. This is fine."

Ophelia nodded and disappeared through the swinging door. Laura spooned sugar into her coffee, then stirred the black liquid thoughtfully.

"I saw Candice yesterday."

"Candice?" Suzanne's voice had a note of wary interest.

Temple darted a glance at Zachary, but the newspaper hid his face from her.

"Yes; she's back on the island. She asked about you, Zachary."

"Did she?" The newspaper remained in place, and his tone was only mildly curious.

"Yes. She'd heard about your marriage and she said she was anxious to meet Temple." Laura looked at Temple now. "Candice is an old flame of Zack's. You'll like her. Don't you think Temple will like Candice, Zack?"

The newpaper rustled as Zack lowered it so that his eyes could meet Laura's. "What is this leading up to, Laura?"

Laura gave him a surprised, innocent look and started to speak, but Ophelia's entrance interrupted her.

"Mr. Stevens, there's a call for you. A Mr. Johnson."

"Oh, thank you." Clifford looked relieved as he dropped his napkin beside his plate and stood. "Excuse me."

"I think I'll go upstairs and freshen up," Suzanne announced, then stood and looked uncertainly at the three still remaining.

Zachary also stood, folded the newspaper, then cast Laura a quelling glance. "If you'll excuse me, ladies, I have some work to do. And, Mother, Temple and I won't be home tonight; we're going out on the yacht." Without waiting for a reaction, he turned and stalked away.

Temple's fork clattered to her plate, and she stared at his departing back. She looked at Suzanne and saw the woman's wide smile.

"That's wonderful! You'll have a marvelous time!" Suzanne patted Temple's shoulder. "You

112

two need to get away for a while." She looked at Laura. "Enjoy your fishing trip, dear; see you later." She followed Zack from the room.

Temple slumped back in her chair. She felt stunned. Why was Zack taking her on a cruise? The thought both excited and frightened her. We'll be alone on that yacht, she thought. All alone.

"You two aren't getting along, are you?"

The other woman's voice interrupted Temple's thoughts and she said confusedly, "What?"

"You're not getting along very well with Zack, are you?"

Temple shrugged. "We're getting along fine."

Laura laughed and shook her head. "You're not fooling anyone, Temple. It doesn't surprise me, though. He didn't get along with Giselle, either."

Temple cringed. How I *hate* to be compared to that woman, she thought. I'm *me!* She looked at Laura and tried to keep her voice steady. "I am not Giselle, so please don't compare us."

"Compare you!" Laura laughed again. "There's no comparison. Why, comparing you and Giselle is like comparing night and day! Giselle was blond, with green eyes, and you have that jet-black hair and those light blue eyes. Not to mention that Giselle was from a good family and was quite a sophisticate and—"

"Laura, please!" With great effort Temple forced herself to lower her voice. "Let's drop the subject, okay?"

Laura shrugged and sipped her coffee. She was silent for a few minutes; then she covered

Temple's hand with her own. False concern was etched on her face.

"I know how it is—he ignored Giselle, too. You see, he's just the type of man who wants something until he gets it, then . . ." She shrugged. "Then, he doesn't want it anymore and he goes back to his former way of life."

Temple gave Laura a long, cool stare. "What do you mean—his former way of life?"

Again Laura shrugged expressively. "Candice."

Temple's heart hammered painfully against her rib cage. That woman again! she thought. She keeps popping up like a bad omen! "Candice?" She looked questioningly at Laura.

"Yes. Candice knows how to handle Zachary." Laura tapped her fingers on her forehead. "She's smart. She knows that Zachary loves a chase, so she just lets him keep chasing her. Once he tired of Giselle, and that was in no time at all, he went back to chasing Candice."

"And you're suggesting that he's tired of me and is ready to start chasing Candice again, is that it?" Temple leaned forward and gave Laura a challenging stare.

"Well, I don't know for sure, of course, but I wouldn't be surprised."

Temple took a deep breath and shook her head slowly. "Laura, why don't you worry about your own marriage and let me worry about mine?" Temple would never have believed she could sound so sarcastic, but she had taken just enough from Laura not to care what the other woman thought.

Laura looked startled and then she clamped her teeth together and glared at Temple. Anger sparked in her eyes, and Temple felt a touch of pride at seeing Laura's face flush hotly.

"Temple!"

Temple quivered at the anger in Zack's voice and turned woodenly to face him. He strode into the room and stood beside her chair, legs planted firmly apart. Temple looked up into his face and wondered if he had overhead her conversation with Laura.

"Pack a bag. We sail in an hour."

"Where to?" Her voice sounded weak in contrast to his deep baritone.

"Just around St. Thomas and St. John, maybe. We can't be gone long; I have to be back here Monday." He glanced at Laura. "I thought you were going fishing?"

"I am." Laura shot him a speculative glance, stood, and walked slowly toward the door. She gave Temple a measured glance from the doorway. "Have fun," she said, though her tone implied that she thought they would have anything but.

Temple pushed her chair back and stood, addressing Zack. "Should I just pack casual clothes?"

"Better include an evening dress. We might stop at a restaurant for dinner." She could read nothing in his tone.

Temple nodded and brushed past him. She sighed with relief, sure that he hadn't heard any of the previous conversation.

Upstairs, she threw several outfits into a suitcase and packed some toiletries, then dressed in shorts and a white terry-cloth shirt. She tried not to think about the coming hours—and night—but it seemed impossible not to. Despite the way he had treated her, her feelings for Zack hadn't changed. She realized that, with only the slightest encouragement, she could fall completely in love with him. Instead, she was left to deal with the ghost of Giselle—and with the apparently very real Candice.

She looked down and saw that her hands were shaking. The conversation with Laura had upset her more than she had known, she realized. She didn't know what to think of Zack—or what he thought of her. Now that Candice was coming back, was he sorry that he had made Temple his bride? And, since they were married, didn't the icy manner they wore with each other bother him, too?

He could certainly be cold when he wanted to be, she thought. Hadn't he proved that over the past two weeks? He was a master of the art. She opened her eyes and stared at the bed before her. Of course, if what Laura had said was true, he had plenty of practice at freezing out his wife.

She recalled his curt, cold manner when she had asked about Giselle. As if—as if he had no feeling for her at all, Temple thought. And what of Candice? How does she fit into all of this? *Is* he seeing her? Is she . . . ?

"Are you ready?"

Temple jumped at the voice behind her. She whirled to face Zachary. "Must you sneak up on me?"

He gave her a quizzical look, the ice in his eyes gone for the first time in weeks. "Are you okay?"

"Yes." She felt some of her anger dissipate at the real concern in his voice. "I'm just . . . confused."

"Oh?" He shoved his hands into his jeans pockets. "Why?"

"I can't figure out why you're taking me away for the weekend."

He shrugged and examined the carpet at his feet. "Because I want to."

"But you've hardly spoken to me in two weeks! Why now?"

His gaze lifted to meet hers, and Temple saw his eyes darken almost to midnight black. "Do you want me to start . . . approaching . . . you again?"

She bit her bottom lip and stalled for a moment or two. "I—I don't know."

"You don't know?" he mocked.

Temple felt completely frustrated in the face of his composure. "Yes! I told you—you're confusing me!"

"*I'm* confusing *you*?" He strode toward her and gripped her upper arms with fingers of steel.

Temple tilted her head back, then sucked in her breath when she saw the sensual light deep in his eyes. She felt her knees grow weak as she stared into those dark eyes. His mouth tensed, as if eager to taste her lips; then he shook his head and pushed her away.

"When you make up your mind what it is you want, let me know. In the meantime, meet me in the foyer in ten minutes."

Temple turned away and crossed quickly to the windows. Cautiously she peeked back over her shoulder and sighed in relief when she saw that Zack had left the room.

She was angry and humiliated at the way he could toy with her emotions. She had wanted him to kiss her a moment ago—and he had known it. But because he had decided to stop, she had been forced to stop, too. She should have known from the beginning how it would be. He led, and everyone else just followed in his wake.

Well, she was going to be different. She had never been a follower and she wasn't going to start now!

She squared her shoulders with new conviction. I won't be as easy to get rid of as Giselle was! she vowed silently. Unfortunately for him, he married a woman with a mind of her own, and for as long as we're married I won't play second fiddle to anyone—especially Candice!

Saint's Escape shimmered, miragelike, atop the blue water that licked at her sides. Her white smokestack was circled by bands of deep maroon and light brown. The St. James crest rested on the bow, and *Saint's Escape* was boldly lettered on the stern.

A white-haired man in a white uniform gave Temple a wide, welcoming smile as she neared the gangplank. He offered Temple his broad hand for balance, and Temple looked at his deeply tanned face and smiled her thanks.

"Welcome aboard, Mrs. St. James." His voice

was a deep baritone and slightly accented, though she couldn't place it.

"Temple, this is Captain Carlos Rosetti," Zachary said as he came up behind her.

"Hello, Captain." Temple withdrew her hand from his and glanced around. Why had she ever imagined that this yacht would be small? she wondered. She should have known that Zachary would never do anything by halves. She turned back to the captain. "How big is *Saint's Escape*?"

"Two hundred and twelve feet, Mrs. St. James."

Temple's eyes widened and she swallowed.

"Have the other guests arrived, Carlos?"

"They are aboard, sir."

Temple turned to her husband. "Other guests?"

Zachary nodded and placed a firm hand on her elbow, propelling her along the deck. "Yes. I've invited William and Mary Eustes. You don't mind, do you?"

Mind? Temple smiled to herself. She was glad, did he but know it. "No, no, I don't mind," she told Zachary. "Where are you pushing me?"

He frowned slightly. "To our quarters. We'll freshen up before we welcome our guests."

Temple smiled and nodded at the young men they passed. Each man wore a T-shirt that had *Saint's Escape* lettered on it in maroon.

"Watch your step," Zachary cautioned as he guided her toward a flight of stairs. She paused once she reached the bottom, her breath all but stopped by the sight of a heavy wood door with a gold plaque engraved MR. AND MRS. Z. ST. JAMES.

"Our quarters," he said emotionlessly, then motioned for her to enter.

She took a few steps inside and then stopped to let her eyes sweep over the elegantly appointed room, done in white and accented with the familiar maroon and tan. An oval table and two chairs were nestled in an alcove near two portholes, and a queen-size bed stood against one wall. It looked like a luxurious hotel room, except for the portholes and subtle reminders, like a ship's clock. Even the dressers were heavy antiques that would have fit equally well in a presidential suite.

Temple crossed the room and opened a door near the dressers. White marbled walls met her gaze and she stepped onto thick white carpet. She let her gaze roam over the double sinks, sunken bathtub and roomy shower stall before she turned to face Zack again.

"Everything satisfactory, Mrs. St. James?" If she hadn't known better, she would have thought he sounded uncertain, even worried. But that could hardly be true, she decided as she took in his long body, leaning indolently against the doorjamb, his powerful frame virtually filling it.

"It's lovely. I had no idea your yacht would be so—so luxurious!"

"Aren't all yachts luxurious?"

"I don't know. I've never been on one before."

He smiled and moved out of the doorframe, allowing her a path of escape. "Dress is casual. All passengers are expected at lunch and dinner; otherwise"—his shoulders lifted in a shrug—"your time is your own aboard the *Escape*."

"What's expected of me as hostess?" Temple asked, edging carefully past him.

Restraining fingers curved around her arm. Zachary's eyes looked like velvet as he turned them to her upturned face, and his voice was softly seductive. "All that is expected of you is to be yourself. Warm, loving, and spirited."

Temple watched his face blur as his mouth descended to meet hers. His lips moved against hers, gently searching for a response.

Every nerve in her body screamed at her to yield to Zack's gentle seduction, but an inner voice reminded her of the way he manipulated people, and of the fact that this marriage was only a business deal between them. She saw herself as a puppet, dangling limply from her strings while, above her, Zachary held those strings, forcing her to move at his will. She stiffened her resolve and held herself erect, refusing to respond to his kiss.

Zachary lifted his head, and she raised her lashes to study his angry, confused expression.

"Tell me, Temple; just when did you decide that I repulsed you?" His voice was soft, yet chilling.

"Y-you don't repulse me." Temple berated herself for the tremor in her voice.

"Then why won't you kiss me back?"

"I—I don't know."

A frown puckered his brow, and the fingers on her arm tightened their hold. In the distance, she heard a lilting chime, and Zachary suddenly released her and walked away. He ran a hand through his dark hair in a gesture of frustration and said coldly, "Those were the chimes; lunch is ready. Let's go." Underneath the anger Temple almost thought she heard a note of pain, and she felt her heart constrict at the sound. For an instant she wanted to run to him and hold him close. She yearned to hear the muffled beat of his heart and feel the warm strength of his enbrace.

"Zachary . . ." She paused and bit her lip.

A bitter smile touched his mouth. "Don't make promises you can't keep, Temple."

Her eyes smarted and she blinked to contain the moisture that gathered there. Zachary's gaze was locked on her face, and as she looked at him she felt her bottom lip tremble.

With a muffled oath, he reached for her and pulled her against his chest. Temple rubbed her cheek against the silk of his shirt and closed her eyes. His heart beat in her ear, just as she had imagined.

Zachary pressed his lips to the top of her head, and Temple felt him tremble. She sighed and wrapped her hands around his waist.

"What's the matter, Temple? Won't you talk to me about it?" His breath stirred her hair.

She swallowed the emotion that had lodged

itself in her throat. "I just need a little time, Zack. I'm confused and I feel out of my element. Everything is so strange. Sometimes you seem like a stranger, someone I never met before."

She felt his chest rise as he took a deep breath before he pushed her gently away. He took her hand and led her toward the door. "I'm trying to understand, Temple, but my patience and will-power have limits. Let's forget the whole thing for now and just go to lunch and greet our passengers."

The bright sun greeted Temple as she emerged from the shadows of the interior to the upper deck. Zachary's hand on the small of her back urged her to the left.

"We're lunching on the Capri Deck," he said close to her ear.

"The Capri Deck?" Temple glanced over her shoulder at him and saw pinpoints of sunlight dance in his dark pupils.

"Straight ahead, songbird."

A pleasant feeling curled inside her when she heard the endearment from his lips. She lifted her chin and quickened her step. For the first time she felt confident in her new role as the wife of Zachary St. James.

A white table had been set on the stern deck, and a maroon-, brown-, and white-striped canopy provided shelter from the sun. Temple smiled when she saw William rise from one of the canvas chairs. She nodded to Mary and then focused on the third person at the table. Her smile faded slightly as she realized how beautiful the woman was—and wondered who she could be. After all, Zack had only mentioned two guests.

Temple heard Zachary's quick intake of breath and she knew then that the third guest had been unexpected.

"Temple!" William squeezed her hand. "So good of you to have us aboard. Hello, Zack." He glanced at the extra woman, then back at Zachary. "I hope you don't mind that we brought Candice along."

"Of course not." Zachary nodded at the woman and turned to Temple. "Temple, this is Candice Franklin, Mary's cousin. Candice, my wife, Temple."

The woman's sleek brown eyebrows rose and her rose-colored lips twitched into a smile. Temple watched bits of sunlight play in the red and gold highlights of her hair and she wondered if the light in her topaz-colored eyes was that of amusement or curiosity.

So this is Candice, Temple thought, as she examined the woman more thoroughly and noted the fawn slacks that accentuated her long legs and the bright orange silk shirt. The blouse had a deep v-neck that exposed the tops of her creamy breasts. How dare she come here! Temple fumed. The nerve! With great effort she managed to smile at the other woman.

"Hello, Candice. Nice to meet you—at last."

"Hello." The topaz eyes focused on a point above Temple's head. "Thanks for having me aboard, Zack."

At the obvious snub, Temple curled her hands

into fists. She tried to think of something cutting to say, but Zack cleared his throat and spoke first.

"Let's eat, shall we?" He stepped around Temple and held a chair out for her.

Uneasiness edged its way into Temple's mind as she studied Candice. She saw the possessive way Candice was eyeing Zack and felt a stab of jealousy, so sharp that it surprised her. Surely she hadn't done something stupid like fall in love with her husband? There must be something going on between the two of them, she thought. Had Candice invited herself aboard so that she could check out the woman who had snatched Zachary from under her well-shaped nose? Or—Temple felt her heart beat irregularly—*have* I really stolen him? Maybe Laura's right, and Candice is here to let me know that she still has a firm hold on my husband.

A man in a brown waistcoat over a white shirt and pants served them lunch. Temple felt her stomach growl with longing when she spied the smoked salmon, asparagus tips, and fried papaya chips.

"Ronald, you can tell Captain Rosetti that we can sail in an hour."

"Yes, sir, Mr. St. James." The man bowed slightly from the waist and disappeared, presumably to pass the order on. When he returned he stood by the rail, his eyes flitting from one person to another in search of an empty glass or plate.

"How many crewmen do you have now, Zack?" Mary asked before tasting the meal.

"Fourteen. How's the salmon?"

"Delicious!" Mary smiled in appreciation.

"Where did you go for your honeymoon?" Candice's topaz gaze was on Zachary's face as she cut the other woman off.

"We're on our honeymoon," Zack replied, his dark eyes moving to Temple's face momentarily. "We were at Saint's Summit for a couple of weeks so Temple could get settled in, then decided to sail around the island this weekend."

"A strange choice for a honeymoon, isn't it?" Candice's voice was almost a purr.

"Not really. Temple is new to the island, and I want her to become familiar with her home."

"What I meant was, I should think you'd want to be alone," Candice purred, her golden gaze moving to Temple's face.

"We have the rest of our lives to be alone. Besides, Temple and I enjoy having our friends with us, don't we, darling?"

Temple almost choked on the salmon when the endearment registered in her mind. Her heart seemed to accelerate when her eyes locked with his. If only he had meant it, she thought to herself. Aloud, she said, "Yes. It's wonderful having all of you here with us."

Zack took her hand in his, and the warmth of his smile brought a flush to her cheeks. Her lashes fluttered down, and she turned shyly away to hide her embarrassment. When his thumb moved to caress the inside of her wrist she almost thought her heart would burst. But when she lifted her lashes her heart seemed to turn to stone as she encountered Candice's cold, hard glare.

The conversation became general once again and remained that way throughout the rest of the meal. But though the food was as delicious as Mary had said, Temple found that her appetite had all but disappeared in the face of her anxieties about Candice. Eventually it seemed to be over, and Temple hoped that Zack would make their excuses, because she badly wanted to get away from Candice. Instead, he leaned back in his chair, reached into his pocket, and withdrew a cigarette. Appearing from nowhere, it seemed, Ronald was at his shoulder. A lighter flared, and Zachary bent his head to touch the tip of his cigarette to the proffered flame.

"Thank you, Ronald." He turned back to his guests. "Did everyone get enough to eat?"

"I'm stuffed," William said, patting his stomach.

Mary laughed at her husband. "How William loves this yachting life!"

"I love Felix's meals, myself," Candice said, with an arch look at Zachary.

"Felix?" Temple asked.

"Felix. Your chef, of course." Candice's smile was indulgent.

"I've been remiss, I'm afraid, in not introducing Temple to the entire crew." Zachary exhaled a cloud of smoke and his dark gaze rested on Candice. "We boarded late, and I wanted to show her our cabin first."

The other woman's smile turned as hard as

the jewels she wore, and she cleared her throat and fastened her eyes on Ronald. "Ronald!" The tone was imperious. "I'd like some wine!"

"Of course, Miss Franklin. Forgive me," he said as he moved swiftly to her side, pouring the golden liquid into her glass.

"Thank you." Candice eyed her plate. "And you may take this away," she snapped, her hand waving in a dismissive gesture. "I've quite lost my appetite."

"Surely you're not seasick?" Zachary's smile was mocking.

"No." Candice's lips curved in a sultry smile aimed directly at Zachary. "You know better than that, darling. After all the trips we've taken on *Saint's Escape,* you should know that I'm quite at home on the water."

Temple slid her gaze to Zachary and saw his eyes narrow and the warning twitch of a muscle in his jaw. But he ignored the other woman's innuendo and said only, "We're ready for dessert, Ronald. Tell Captain Rosetti we can set sail now."

Temple was sure that Zack's soft tone was a smoke screen. She examined him out of the corner of her eye and wondered why he was so upset. Was he feeling uncomfortable? He must not like having his wife and his mistress meet, she thought with a twinge of malice. He wasn't the type of man who would sit still to be made to look the fool.

Dessert was placed in front of her, and Temple spooned the honeydew melon into her mouth and searched for a neutral topic. The highly charged atmosphere was wearing on her nerves. Then she felt the floor beneath her begin to vibrate and heard the distant hum of a motor. They were under way, which at least gave her something to talk about even if it now made escape impossible.

"I'm looking forward to this," Temple addressed Mary. "I was telling Zachary earlier that this is a beautiful craft."

"Yes, we're quite envious of you both." Mary smiled at Temple, and Temple thought she caught a flicker of understanding in the older woman's eyes. "We'd buy one, but they're so expensive to keep up."

"Why should we buy one when we have a generous friend like Zack?" William asked with a chuckle.

"Sometimes I think that Zack is too generous—generous to a *fault*, if you know what I mean." Candice looked pointedly at Temple.

The piece of melon she was eating suddenly refused to slide down Temple's throat, and she reached for her wine. The liquid forced the melon down, and she felt tears sting the corners of her eyes as she coughed.

Zachary placed a hand on her shoulder and leaned forward, an expression of concern covering his previously impassive features. "Temple? Are you all right?"

Temple nodded and moved away from his touch. How could he? she thought. Candice must actually know of the arrangement concerning their marriage. The thought made her feel sick.

"Mr. St. James?" Ronald stood beside Zachary's chair.

"Yes, Ronald?"

"Captain Rosetti would like a word with you, sir."

"Very well." Zachary gave Temple a questioning look before he stood. "Excuse me, please."

Temple watched the graceful sway of his shoulders as he walked toward the bow of the craft and felt torn between the desire to run after him and beg his forgiveness and the need to confront him with her anger, to find out what he had told Candice about their arrangement.

"I hope it's not bad news."

"Bad news?" Temple turned to face Mary.

"We heard that there's a hurricane forming."

"A hurricane!" Temple's eyes widened. "Right here?"

"Out at sea," William answered. "The direction hadn't been established at the last report."

"Oh, dear!" Temple gasped and looked in the direction Zachary had disappeared.

Candice's laughter grated on her stretched nerves. "My dear! You look sick! Don't let a little hurricane bother you so. You'll get used to them—*if* you're here long enough."

Temple forced herself to turn a steady gaze on Candice. "I do feel a little sick. But not because of the hurricane," she added silently. She held the other woman's eyes for a moment and relished the quick anger she saw there. Then she deliberately turned her back on Candice, excused herself to Mary and William, and walked away.

Chapter Seven

Temple felt better after a quick walk around the deck. After a few minutes she returned to the stern and sat in a deck chair to watch Mary and William play backgammon. She noticed Candice had disappeared. She put on a pair of large sunglasses and rested her head against the back of the chair.

The bright sun warmed her skin, and she was soon lost in thought. If she had known what the future held, would she still have married Zack? Yes, she was forced to admit, she would have, and not entirely to help her parents. And speaking of Zack, what was keeping him? Bad news about the hurricane? Newspaper accounts of fatalities and devastating winds and tides flashed through her mind. She shivered and forced the bleak thoughts aside.

A husky laugh sounded behind her, and she turned in her seat to see Candice and Zachary walking toward her. Candice's hand was tucked in the crook of Zachary's arm, and her topaz eyes were fixed possessively on his face. Temple felt a sharp, jealous pain slice through her and she sat straighter in the chair.

"Anything wrong, Zack?" William looked up from the game board. "News about the hurricane?"

Zachary disengaged himself from Candice. "I was just telling Candice that the hurricane is, in fact, heading for St. Thomas."

"And you're laughing?" Mary turned surprised eyes on Candice.

"Not about the hurricane." Candice shook her glimmering hair. "Zack and I were . . ." —the golden gaze slid to Temple for a moment—". . . discussing something else."

Zachary sat down next to Temple, a worried frown creasing his brow. "If it doesn't change direction or speed, the hurricane should reach the island by Tuesday or Wednesday. Not good, is it?"

"I should say not!" William leaned back in his chair, suddenly uninterested in the backgammon game. "Should we start back now?"

"Oh, no!" Candice's expression registered dismay. "It's not that serious, is it, Zack?"

"Captain Rosetti is keeping a close watch. He'll notify me if conditions worsen." Zack leaned his head against the back of the chair, and his dark gaze swept the blue horizon. "I just spoke with Mother. She and Clifford are in San Juan preparing for the maiden voyage of *The Mermaid*. I told them to stay put until further notice."

"You're canceling the trip?" William asked.

"No, just postponing it. I contacted Samson and suggested that he have his family meet him in San Juan. Maybe you should all think about doing the same."

Candice sat down and crossed her legs to show off her golden tan. Her irritation was plain as she said, "Really, Zack. Don't you think maybe you're overreacting?"

Zachary tossed her an impatient look. "We'll see, Candice. If that hurricane does hit the island, it won't be any picnic, I can assure you." His eyes narrowed and he looked at William. "Tomorrow we'll drop you and Mary off. I'd suggest that you fly out of here as soon as possible."

William nodded and covered his wife's hand with his own. "We'll fly to St. Martin and visit your sister. How's that?"

"That sounds fine, darling."

"What about you, Zack? Where will you hide out?" Candice asked.

"Oh, I'll stay at Saint's Summit. I want to keep an eye on things." He paused, then added, "Temple, I think you'd better join Mother and the rest of the family in San Juan."

"But I—" The protest died abruptly when Zachary's hand took hers in a steely grip and his eyes darkened with warning. She swallowed and promised herself that she'd talk to him alone.

"I think I'll stay on the island, too," Candice said with a smile.

"Don't be a fool, Candice," Zachary told her. "You'd better make other plans."

"But you're staying."

"I've been through hurricanes before, and I can stay in the shelter behind the house."

"Is the shelter big enough for two?" Candice gave him a sly look.

Temple bit her bottom lip and lowered her lashes. She refused to let Candice or Zack see the fury she felt. Zack's fingers curled more tightly around Temple's and she wondered if he was cautioning her to curb her tongue.

"If I wanted company, Candice, I would have asked my wife to stay with me." His voice was soft but firm, and Temple felt a thrill of confidence surge through her.

She lifted her lashes and met Candice's cold eyes, and the confidence quickly faded. How could she feel confident when this woman remained as a barrier to her happiness? She wanted to make her marriage work, but how could she? Hadn't Candice had a head start? How many years had Zachary known this woman? Was Candice as smart as Laura had said? Candice—always keeping her distance, waiting now in the wings for Zachary to tire of this marriage that was really nothing more than a simple business agreement and come back to the excitement of their affair.

"Who's winning, William?" Zachary's question interrupted Temple's thoughts, and she forced herself to focus on the here and now.

William blinked, then stared at the board. "Mary, I think."

"Not for long," Mary said with a laugh. "He always beats me."

William gave Mary a loving look, then studied the board again. Temple felt envy well up inside her. How wonderful it must be to have such a firm foundation for a marriage, such trust and mutual affection. She longed for such stability in her own life so much that she actually hurt. Abruptly she pushed herself up from the chair.

"I think I'll go sit in the sun for a while," she said in response to Zachary's questioning expression.

"You can swim if you'd like," he suggested.

"Swim?" Temple looked out at the blue-green ocean.

Zachary laughed at her confusion. "We have a pool aboard, Temple. Just ask one of the deckhands to direct you."

"Oh. Thank you." Temple smiled and hurried from the deck, feeling like a fool. What must Mary and William think of her? And Candice! She found the staircase that led down to the cabins and ran quickly down the stairs.

Once inside the master cabin she sat on the bed and shook her head. Candice and a hurricane! What else could possibly happen to her? Her hands smoothed the maroon bedspread and a shiver of apprehension raced through her. Was Zachary planning on sleeping here—with her? Just because he had left her alone at Saint's Summit it didn't necessarily follow that he meant to do so here. The thought made her jump to her feet, and she stared at the bed. A bed made for two.

She backed away from it and then turned and rummaged through the dresser until she found her swimsuit. She went into the bathroom and quickly changed into the one-piece lime-green suit, then studied herself in the full-length mirror on the back of the door. The deep V-neck exposed the smooth skin between her breasts, and the leg openings were cut high. Too high? Temple wondered as she turned sideways to survey the length of her legs. Her eyes moved to examine the low-cut back. She shrugged. I've worn this all over San Juan, she thought. Why am I questioning the style now?

Because Zachary St. James is going to be looking at me, she answered herself. He's going to notice every little detail.

She turned from the mirror and opened the door. She froze when she saw the lean male form stretched out on the bed.

"I—I didn't hear you come in."

Zachary raised his head, and his eyes glistened as they swept over her figure. "I decided to take a nap. Want me to show you where the pool is?

"No, that's okay. You rest."

"I like your swimsuit." An appreciative smile curved his lips. "You're the loveliest woman aboard."

Temple leaned a shoulder against the doorframe and aimed her words carefully at him. "I'm sure that Candice wouldn't agree."

His gaze narrowed. "I didn't invite her, you know."

"It doesn't seem that she needs an invitation. She's quite at home here."

He sighed and stared at the ceiling. "I don't

want to argue about this. Not when you look so beautiful."

"I'm not looking for an argument," Temple persisted. "I'm looking for an explanation. I want to know where I stand."

He propped himself up on his elbows. "So you want to know where you stand, hmmm?" He gave her a wry smile. "Funny—I've been wondering where I stand with you."

Temple met his gaze. "I asked first."

"Very well." He glanced at the ceiling, as if he were thinking about his words before he spoke them. When his eyes met hers again, Temple saw naked honesty reflected there. "We're married. I want you, but you keep telling me that you're confused about your feelings for me, so I've been attempting to leave you alone to find your feet, to be patient and understanding." His eyes darkened. "I don't know how long I can keep that up. I know that I behaved badly that first night, but you provoked me." He held up a hand when she started to protest, then swallowed and lowered his voice. "Where do you stand? Well, that depends entirely on you. It seems to be out of my hands."

Temple took a deep breath. "And what about Candice? Do you still . . . enjoy her company?"

"Enjoy her company?" He seemed to taste each word. "Yes, I suppose I do. Why do you keep mentioning her? Are you jealous?"

Temple winced inwardly as his words struck home. "Of course I'm not jealous. I just refuse to have you flaunt her in my face!"

Irritation flitted across his features. "I told you

that I didn't invite her!" He frowned, then said grimly, "You see? We're arguing, just like we always do." Slowly, he held out a hand to her, and his tone was commanding. "Come here."

Passion darkened his eyes, and Temple hesitated. She looked at him and felt a strange tugging at her heart that seemed to pull her toward him. Almost without being aware of it, she crossed the room and laid her hand in his. She watched his tanned fingers curl around hers and thought how small her hand seemed in contrast to his.

His other hand moved to the soft skin of her back and his fingers brushed against her until goose bumps raced over her body. Lazily he moved his hand over her waist, finally letting it rest along her hip. Temple forced her eyes to meet his, and her breath caught in her throat when she saw the dark glint of his pupils. The sight sent her thoughts reeling back to that night at Drake's Seat, and she shivered.

Suddenly he tugged at her hand, pulling her off balance, and she fell across him. He twisted her around so that his mouth could find hers.

Gently his lips worked against hers in a seductive caress. Temple closed her eyes and felt desire for him course through her. His arms closed around her and he deepened his kiss. Temple's lips parted and she felt the tip of his tongue skim over them before it touched her own.

A longing she had never known filled her, and she shifted her weight to mold her body closer to his. She fumbled with the buttons of his shirt until they finally gave way and she could run her hands over his smooth skin. She felt the muscles in his back and shoulders ripple beneath her hungry fingers as he held her closer still.

Then Zachary rolled, pinning her beneath him, and his mouth claimed her cheeks, her eyelids, her throat. She opened her eyes and smiled when she saw his dark head and felt his lips and tongue tracing moist circles on the skin between her breasts. She burrowed her fingers in the silkiness of his hair and sighed.

Her emotions were like a whirlpool, sucking her deeper and deeper into its vortex. Finally the swirling sensations merged into one, and Temple breathed Zachary's name as if calling upon him to complete her dizzy journey.

He lifted his lips from her and raised himself so that he could look down into her face. He smiled and kissed the tip of her nose. "You're far more beautiful than Candice, songbird."

Temple's answering smile froze on her lips. She fell with a crash from the lofty heights of emotion. Candice!

She shoved at his shoulders, then slipped from beneath him. "How *dare* you compare me to—to—her!" She shook with anger as she stood and stared at him.

He shook his head, as if trying to clear it. "What? What are you babbling about? Come back here."

"I will not! You're going to have to make a choice!" She pointed a shaking finger at him, then took several steps back as he reached for her. "No! I won't be like Giselle!"

His eyes became obsidian pools. "Explain that statement!"

"I don't have to explain; you already know what I'm talking about! Candice is your mistress, and there's no use in your denying it!"

Temple stepped further away when she saw fury tighten his jaw and flame in his eyes.

"Why should I deny it when you've already found me guilty?" His voice was granite hard. He pushed himself from the bed and stood to tower over her.

Temple felt small and weak beside him, and her voice shook when she warned him, "Don't you lay a hand on me, Zachary! I warn you, I'll—I'll . . ." She choked back the rest of the sentence when she saw the determined gleam in his eyes.

"I'm your husband!" His fingers dug into the flesh of her upper arms. "I have every right to put my hands on you!"

Temple winced at the pain and the angry tone of his voice. "You have no right to . . ."

Suddenly the room swam as the hands on her shoulders shook her, then flung her on the bed as if she were a rag doll.

Temple blinked up at the man who was her husband and she shivered under his chilling gaze.

"Don't challenge me, Temple!" His voice quivered with rage. "And don't threaten me! I'm tired of your teasing ways and childish games! I've given you time to adjust—plenty of time—and I'm not going to give you much more!"

Tears welled in her eyes, blurring his face, and she drew a breath that broke in a sob.

Zachary turned sharply on his heel and strode to the door. He turned to her before he left the room and his tone was cold.

"I'm staying here tonight, Mrs. St. James—with you—and I don't care whether you like the idea or not!"

Temple raised her chin and met his eyes. "Why me? Why don't you grace Candice with your presence?"

A bitter smile lifted one corner of his mouth. "You'd like that, wouldn't you? Too bad, Temple; see you tonight."

He slammed the door, and Temple collapsed on the bed. Sobs rose in her throat, and she muffled the sounds against the spread as she gave herself up to her misery.

The eerie creaking of the ship penetrated the fog that shrouded Temple's mind. Gradually her lids fluttered up to focus on the dimly lit room. The motion beneath her chased away the final residue of sleep, and she stretched. Her limbs stiffened as her gaze was arrested by the shadowy figure of a man seated across from her.

Her lips formed his name, yet no sound escaped through her clenched teeth. Zachary didn't move, and Temple gingerly propped herself on her elbows and squinted into the dusk. No black glitter from his pupils reached her, and she realized that he was asleep. His head leaned to one side, and she could see the black lashes resting on his cheeks. The steady sound of his breathing reached her, and she relaxed against the pillows. Her senses told her that the yacht was moving quickly, and she wondered if their plans had changed since this afternoon.

What time was it? she wondered. Her eyes found the clock by the bed. Four o'clock. Dawn would greet them soon.

She thought back to the hours she had spent waiting anxiously in bed for the sound of footsteps outside in the hall. Finally, after hours of jumping at the slightest noise, she had fallen asleep. Her eyes returned to Zack. When had he slipped into the room? And why was he sleeping in the chair?

A light tapping sounded on the door, and Zack stirred, then opened his eyes. His ebony gaze rested on her and he frowned.

"Yes? Who is it?" he called.

"Rogers, sir. The captain needs you." The voice was muffled by the thickness of the door.

Zachary straightened in the chair and ran a hand through his hair. "Very well. I'm coming."

Temple pulled the sheet up under her chin and watched as Zachary rose from the chair. He bent and picked up a windbreaker from the floor, then moved toward the door.

"When you say your prayers, Temple, just be thankful for this terrible weather." Zachary paused at the door and thrust his arms into the sleeves of the windbreaker. "Mother Nature has saved you from your fate tonight. I have too much to worry about without bothering with the likes of you." He wrenched open the door and left the room, slamming it behind him.

Temple stared at the closed door and wondered if what she felt could be disappointment. What was wrong with her? she asked herself. She clutched the sheet tighter and stared at the wall, waiting for dawn to cast its pink glow before she scrambled from the bed and dressed. Standing on tiptoe, she looked out the porthole at the churning sea. Droplets of rain splashed on the glass and the sky was a slate gray. A pink hue lay along the horizon, as if promising an end to the bleak weather.

Temple slipped into a slicker and smoothed some light makeup over her soft skin. Dark circles rested under her eyes, evidence of her disturbed night. She added blusher to her pale cheeks, then stroked mascara on her lashes.

She left the room and walked carefully along the hall and up the stairs. The boat rocked beneath her feet and walking was difficult. A light rain misted her face as she emerged from the stairwell. She flattened her palms against the wall and inched toward the cabin where the controls were located. Through a billowing sheet of rain she could see the tall figure of Zachary and a shorter form, which she took to be the captain, as well as several others behind them.

Temple opened the door and was almost flung into the cabin by the force of the wind. Zachary whirled to face her and tossed her an irritated look.

"Why didn't you stay below?"

Temple glanced around the small cabin, but her gaze froze on Candice. The woman sat in one of the chairs, cradling a cup of coffee between her hands. She smiled sweetly at Temple.

Temple frowned and took the towel offered to her by one of the deckhands. She rubbed the rain from her face and hair. She must look terrible.

"I didn't know you'd given orders for me to remain in the cabin," Temple answered, her eyes still locked on Candice.

"Never mind." Zachary turned away from her to stare at the horizon.

Temple followed his gaze and caught her breath when she saw the green peaks of St. Thomas rising from the sea ahead of them.

"We're almost home!"

"Yes." Zachary didn't turn to look at her.

"More coffee, darling?"

Temple gave Candice a killing glance, then looked to Zachary to catch his reaction to the woman's endearment. His back was still toward her and she could tell nothing. She swallowed her anger and stood on tiptoe to look over his shoulder at the choppy water.

"Is the hurricane still headed in this direction?"

"Yes." Zachary turned to look at Candice. "No coffee, thanks." He looked back to the horizon. "The hurricane has increased its speed, though." Now his eyes found Temple. "Look, I suggest you pack. We'll be docking within the hour."

Although the hardness in his eyes sent a cold

jolt through her, Temple stood her ground for a few moments. Finally she managed a smile and said, in a level tone, "Yes, perhaps I'd better."

When Zachary added, "Candice, you'd better go along too," Temple didn't know whether to be sorry at being thrown together with the woman or glad that Zack had sent her away, too.

Temple left the cabin, hurrying to get a head-start on Candice. Holding tight to the rail, she bent her head to the rain and fought the wind to reach the stairwell. She almost ran downstairs, despite the pitching of the boat, then stood and watched water drip from her clothing to form small puddles on the carpet.

"Hope you don't catch your death of cold."

Temple lifted her head to face Candice. "I doubt that I will. I'm a pretty healthy girl."

Candice looked back up the stairwell and sighed. "Poor, dear Zack. I hope he doesn't come down with something. He's had such an awful night." She clicked her tongue sympathetically. "We so wanted this little vacation, and now this terrible weather has destroyed all our plans." Candice looked at Temple again and gave her another false smile.

Temple leaned against the wall trying to look and sound casual as she asked the other woman, "How long have you known Zack?"

Candice looked at the ceiling for an instant, then back at Temple. "Oh, since before he married Giselle. I've weathered many storms with him."

Temple raised her eyebrows slightly. "Oh? Tell me, why is an attractive woman like yourself still unmarried? Don't tell me the man of your choice hasn't asked you?"

Candice laughed. "Oh, my dear! I suppose that marriage sounds wonderful to a girl like yourself, but not to me! I like my present arrangement. I'm not interested in the shackles of marriage." With a flip of her hands, she tossed her red-gold hair back from her shoulders. "I don't *need* a contract to convince me that my man is committed to our relationship."

Temple felt her face burn and realized that her hands were clenched so tightly that her nails were cutting into her palms. She forced her fingers to relax and reached for the doorknob. "That's very interesting, Candice, but some of us view marriage as much more than just a contract. Goodbye." Temple turned and wrenched open the door to the master cabin.

"Hardly goodbye, Temple; I'll see you soon—on the plane."

"What?" Temple stopped and turned to face Candice again.

"Mary and William and I are catching a flight to St. Martin. Zack told me that you'll be joining us."

Temple surveyed the woman through narrowed eyes. "I think not. I prefer to stay on St. Thomas."

"But Zack said that would be out of the question," Candice told her.

"Then I'll go to San Juan—by myself. Excuse me." Temple left the woman and closed the door. She leaned against the solid wall and waited for her anger to diminish.

She was even angrier at Zack than at Candice. How dare he tell that woman that she would join her on a flight to St. Martin? She was not his pet dog, trained to do whatever he wanted her to!

She moved away from the wall and began throwing her clothes into her suitcase. "I'll go to San Juan and I won't come back. I'll never have to see him again!" Even as she spoke them, she knew her threats were empty ones.

Slowly she closed her suitcase and locked it. I can't leave him, she thought. I promised him I'd stay at least a year. And even if I hadn't, what would be the point of leaving? Wherever I go, he'll always be with me.

The sound of the door opening behind her made her spin around. Zachary stood in the threshold, ruffling his hair so that raindrops flew in all directions.

Temple stared at the strands of dark hair that clung to his forehead, and her breath caught in her throat as his masculinity seemed to fill the room.

When his eyebrows met in a frown, Temple shook herself, realizing that she was staring at him. His dark gaze swept over her, then moved to focus on her suitcase. "Are you all packed?"

"Yes." She clasped and unclasped her hands, struggling for an ounce of composure.

"Would you mind packing my things for me? I could send a deckhand, but they're all rather busy right now and I'd like to stay above while we dock. I'm keeping a close ear on the radio to make sure the weather is still good in San Juan."

147

Temple stepped back until she felt the bed against her thighs and stopped. How much did he know? Had he talked to Candice already? "Why are you checking the weather in San Juan?" she asked nervously.

He put his hands on his hips and sighed. "Because my family is there. Remember?"

"Oh," Temple said, relieved. Then: "But I'm supposed to go with Candice and the others to St. Martin. Isn't that right—Master?"

Zack's eyes seemed to glow like coals. He slowly lowered his lids and sighed deeply. "Please, Temple. I'm too tired to fight with you." His smoldering gaze met hers again. "Will you or will you not pack my things?"

Temple saw the lines of exhaustion at the corners of his mouth and eyes. He had been asked to make too many decisions in too little time. She nodded. "Of course I will. How long before we dock?"

"Half an hour." He turned and left the room.

Temple stepped forward and watched his tall form disappear in the shadows of the stairwell; then she turned to the task of packing his belongings.

She began sweeping his clothes from the hangers and folding them. The musky scent of him rose toward her as she handled a shirt he had worn, and she breathed in the male smell. She closed her eyes and saw him as he had been a few minutes ago: tall and compelling as he stood in the doorway, water droplets sparkling like diamonds in his thick brown hair.

The picture faded and reality swept over her. Temple's hands closed tighter around the shirt and she threw it blindly from her. It hit something, and she opened her eyes to see Zachary standing a few feet from her, the shirt resting at his feet.

Temple stifled a gasp and her eyes widened as she faced him. He looked at the shirt, then lifted his gaze to her.

"Why do you fight me, Temple?"

Temple cringed at the softly menacing tone of his voice. "Because I don't want you!" Her voice trembled.

"I see." He bent and retrieved the shirt. "You don't want me—but you do want my money."

Something wild unleashed itself in Temple and sent her running across to him. She pounded the solid wall of his chest, her breath coming in strangled gasps.

"I hate you! I hate you!" The words tore from her throat, and she continued to beat against his wet windbreaker until all the fight in her was extinguished and she fell limply against him.

His fingers wrapped around her wrists and he held her still. Temple listened to the steady beat of his heart and let her sobs dwindle to tiny gasps.

"Finished? Do you feel better now?"

His breath stirred her hair, and she pulled back from him so that she could look at his face. He had a questioning look in his eyes, and a smile lifted one corner of his mouth. Temple swallowed and nodded.

"Very well." He released her. "We're packed? Good; let's go. The sooner we're back on land, the better."

"What about the hurricane?"

"It should hit the island by early tomorrow morning. Come on." He held out his hand to her.

"N-not yet." Temple wiped the tears from her cheeks. "I need to freshen up."

"I'll meet you at the gangplank; don't take long." He swept the luggage from the bed and strode from the room.

Temple let out a shaky breath and walked to the bathroom. The mirror showed her a face washed by tears.

"What's wrong with me?" she asked her reflection. "I don't even know myself anymore. I don't know what I want!" She sighed and stared at the blue-eyed girl in the mirror. "One thing you do know, Temple—you don't hate him."

She turned and left the cabin, making her way to the gangplank where her husband waited for her.

Chapter Eight

Zachary slammed the telephone receiver into the cradle, and Temple jumped.

"Another problem?" she asked nervously. "Nothing's wrong with your mother . . . ?"

"No." His voice was touched by defeat, and he ran a hand through his hair. "No more planes are leaving after five o'clock, and those before are all booked solid. I don't know why I let you talk me out of sending you to St. Martin with Mary and William." He fished a cigarette from his pocket and struck a match. The flame licked at the cigarette tip and he inhaled deeply. "You'll have to stay here . . . with me."

Temple watched the smoke hover around his head like a halo. "I'm sorry."

Again he combed his fingers through his hair, a gesture that Temple was beginning to greet with unwilling affection.

"It's not that I want to be rid of you, Temple. Try to understand." His eyes locked with hers. "I just want you to be safe. A hurricane can be terrible, destroying everything in its path."

"But we have a shelter behind the house." Temple pointed in the direction of the shelter and watched the slow shake of Zachary's head.

"It's small and inadequate. It might do—it will have to, I suppose." One tanned hand reached out to enclose hers. "It won't be very comfortable, and you'll be frightened out of your wits."

Temple's chin lifted. "I won't be!"

Zachary smiled. "Good, then you won't mind if I'm frightened out of mine, will you?"

Temple stared at him and found it impossible to imagine him scared. "You're used to these hurricanes."

"You never gets used to them." He glanced around the sitting room, then dialed a number.

Temple listened as he talked to someone about the weather conditions. By the time the call was completed, worry lines were etched on his forehead.

"We'd better start getting ready." He stood, releasing her hand.

"What should I do?" Temple asked, tilting her head back to look into his face.

"Get all the blankets and flashlights you can find. I'll be out back."

Zachary left her, and Temple went upstairs to fetch the things he wanted. She found three flashlights in the hall closet, then went to her bedroom for blankets. In the dressing room, she opened the cupboards and found four more. Electric blankets.

Temple fingered the electric cords and smiled. These won't be much good if there's no electricity, she thought. She held one to her cheek and rubbed the fuzzy material against her skin. She shrugged. They'll keep the rain out, I suppose.

As she left the dressing room her eyes fell on the huge bed. A shiver raced up her spine. Our bed. The thought lingered in her mind for a few moments. No, my bed. His is in the dressing room. But I've wanted him in here with me, she admitted. I've wanted to feel him next to me.

Shadows played across the bedspread, and Temple looked to the French doors. Outside, the trees were stirring as the wind came up. She roused herself from her thoughtful mood and crossed to the door.

"Got to get these things to Zack," she murmured as she descended the stairs.

The back door was ajar, and she hurried outside. The stone door to the underground shelter was open, and she stood beside it, gazing down the dark stairwell.

"Zack? Zack?"

"Yes. Be up in a minute." His voice came to her from a distance.

Temple shifted from one foot to the other and waited. Finally she saw the top of his head, then his shoulders. He reached for the things she held in her arms.

"Give them here. Want to come down and have a look?"

Templed handed him the pile, then shook her head, suddenly frightened of being so alone with him.

"Come on; don't be afraid." He reached for her hand.

Temple swallowed her fear and allowed his fingers to clasp hers. She stepped down into the darkness. As the dusk enveloped her she paused. Zack pulled her to him, his arm curving around her shoulders.

"Come on, songbird, just two more steps. That's it." His voice was soothing.

Temple stopped as the stairs ended and a beam of light reached across the floor as Zack turned on a flashlight.

"Carpet!" Temple stared at the plush red fabric beneath her feet.

"Yes." Zack chuckled and moved away from her. More light flooded the room as he turned on several ceiling lights. Temple stared, amazed.

"Battery powered." Zack answered her unspoken question and dumped the blankets onto a table.

The room was small and sparsely furnished. Two tables and two chairs were set near one wall, and two pallets lay on the floor nearby. Shelves were built into another wall and stocked with canned goods and other supplies.

"Not as bad as you thought, hmmm?" Zachary sat in one of the chairs and offered her a smile.

"No. I thought it would have bare floors and no lights or furniture or anything." Temple examined the larder. Jugs of water and pouches of dried fruit lined one shelf. Another held canned foods, wine, vitamins, and cooking utensils.

"We keep it well stocked. Most homes in this area don't have shelters, though."

"Why not?"

Zachary shrugged. "They make do or they leave. Shall we secure the house now?"

"Secure the house?" Temple turned from the cupboards to find him standing near the stairs.

"We'll have something to eat, then close the shutters and lock the doors to minimize the possibility of damage."

"How long before the hurricane is due?"

"Not for hours yet, but there's a lot to do first." He motioned for her to precede him, and she headed for the stairs. Sunlight greeted her when she reached the outdoors again, and she blinked at the change in weather.

"It seems to have cleared!" She turned to Zack and smiled.

"Looks can be deceiving, Temple." He moved toward the house without waiting for her, and she followed quickly.

The moon was an orange orb perched on the powder-gray horizon.

Temple stood by the sitting-room windows and watched as the lunar globe gradually lost its vivid color. A brisk breeze stirred the trees; the calm before the storm was ending. Sounds of the shutters being drawn and latched floated to her from upstairs. Suddenly Temple wished she had been able to join the rest of the family in San Juan. Foreboding entered her, and she trembled.

"Hurricane." The word whispered past her lips. The radio reports had been chilling. The broadcasters had reported the numerous deaths and miles of destruction left by previous storms, and each account had added to the fright that burned in Temple's mind.

It's this waiting, she told herself. It would be better if the hurricane would just catch us by surprise.

She shook her head. No, then Zachary couldn't have made all these preparations for their safety. At least this way they had a measure of security.

Zachary's tread sounded on the staircase, and Temple spun away from the window.

"Temple?" His voice carried into the sitting room.

"I'm in here."

He strode through the archway and gave her a sympathetic smile. "Come on away from the window. It isn't safe; I'd hate to see all that glass blow in on you."

Temple sighed and shifted from one foot to the other. "I hate this waiting. I just wish the hurricane would hit and be gone."

Zachary's smile grew. "I know; so do I. You know the saying, though; a watched pot never boils." He extended a hand to her. "Come on; let's get some dinner. I'm starved."

Temple placed her hand in his and felt an immediate sense of security in his strong grip. Strangely, they were getting along better now than they ever had before. She walked beside him to the kitchen.

"Where have the servants gone?"

"To their families. Maybe to the shelters in town." He let go of her hand and walked to the cabinets. "Now, what shall we make? How hungry are you?"

"Not very." Temple sat at the rough wooden table in the center of the large kitchen. She watched as he rummaged through the cabinets, selecting boxes and cans, only to put them back on the shelves again.

"I know!" He snapped his fingers and turned to her. "We'll have my specialty!"

"What's that?" Temple traced the pattern of the wood with her fingers.

"Pepper steak. You can toss a salad, and we'll make some rice. How does that sound?"

"Fine," Temple murmured, suddenly shy in the face of the feelings growing in her. Why had she never realized it before? she wondered. She loved this man. Now, when it was too late and she had ruined any chance for happiness between them, when he cared too little about her to even fight with her, she faced the fact that she loved him as she would never love any other man.

"Temple!"

Her head jerked up as her name exploded harshly from his lips. "What? What is it?"

Zachary shook his head and walked to her chair. He rested a hand on her shoulder, and his dark eyes glinted with reproof. "Come on, now! Snap out of it, will you? Help me make dinner and stop thinking about the weather. We'll get through this in fine shape; you'll see."

His fingers kneaded her flesh, and Temple smiled. "You're right. There's nothing we can do about it, is there?"

"Yes, there is." He turned to the stove and put a large skillet on one of the burners. "We can eat and enjoy ourselves. Will you toss the salad?"

"Of course." Temple rose and went to search the refrigerator for lettuce, tomatoes, green onions, carrots, and radishes. She smiled as she listened to Zachary whistling. The tune was haunting, and Temple searched her memory for its name.

"Zack, what's the name of that tune?"

"What?" He looked up from preparing the steak; then a solemn, withdrawn expression settled on his face. "I don't know. I can't remember."

Temple stared at him and wondered what memory her question had evoked. "Zachary, I didn't mean to upset you."

"You didn't." His words were curt, almost cutting.

Temple flinched inwardly and longed for the return of his previous light mood. She decided not to press the subject and, instead, concentrated on helping to prepare their meal.

Within half an hour Temple had the rice boiling and the salad tossed and had set the table in the sunroom. She lit two candles in the center of the table and watched as the glow of the flames danced upon the dinnerware.

"We're eating in here?"

Temple turned to find Zachary behind her. "Yes. I thought the sunroom would be nicer than the dining room since it's just the two of us."

"Hmmm." Zachary put the steak on the table

and cast her a sly glance. "We can keep an eye on the weather from here, too, can't we?"

Temple smiled. "Caught me, didn't you?"

"Temple, when the hurricane hits we'll be in the shelter. I've told you that it's not due until nearly dawn."

"It can change direction or speed! You told me *that,* too!"

"Yes, but I'm keeping a close watch and I'm listening to radio reports. Don't worry!" He shook his head and returned to the kitchen.

Temple sank into a chair and waited for him to return. She tried to keep her eyes focused on the candles, but she couldn't. As if of its own accord, her look kept returning to the stirring trees outside and the growing darkness.

"Here we are!" Zachary brought the salad and rice to the table. "This salad looks delicious."

Temple tore her gaze from the windows and set her mind to the meal before her. The savory aroma of pepper steak filled her nostrils, and she realized that she was hungry.

"So this is your specialty, is it?"

Zack nodded. "Taste it. Tell me if it's not the best you've ever had."

Temple smiled and tasted the tender meat. She closed her eyes. "Mmmm. It really is the best."

Zachary laughed. "Ah, now *that's* a dutiful wife."

Dutiful wife. Wife. The words penetrated Temple's thoughts. She looked at the man across the table from her. What did she know of him? He was a stranger—this man who was her husband. This man she loved.

"Zachary . . . do you really think of me as your wife?"

The question seemed to startle him. His eyes widened a fraction before his brow creased in thought. "Yes, I do. Why do you ask?"

Temple pushed the salad around in her dish. "I suppose because I really find it hard to think of you as my husband."

"I can rectify that."

Temple refused to meet his gaze, though she could feel his eyes upon her. "You're speaking of sex, I take it?"

"No. I'm speaking of making love."

Her eyes challenged him now. "Do you think I believe you know the difference?"

"I'd like to think so." His eyes softened, matching the tone of his voice.

Temple glanced away from him and sought for firmer ground. "How can I feel I know you when you hide so much from me?"

"Now what are you babbling about?"

"Like when I asked you about that song you were whistling and you snapped my head off!"

He pushed his plate away and reached for a cigarette. The flame of his lighter sent a flicker of light to his ebony eyes. "It's a song from . . . other times."

"With Giselle?"

"Yes." He finished his wine and set the fragile glass on the table with a deliberate motion. His fingers curled around the stem. "Now, what does that tell you about me?"

"Nothing, really." Temple lowered her gaze. "Everyone seemed to like Giselle."

"Yes, well, she worked hard at it."

The bitterness in his voice sent a cold shiver through Temple. She studied him and caught the pain in his eyes.

Zachary lowered his lashes for a moment. When the dark fringe lifted, his eyes were empty, expressionless. "Let's wash up and then go to the shelter. We'll take the radio and some good books with us."

"It will be a long night." Temple waited for his assistance before she rose from the chair.

"In a way, I'm glad you stayed."

Temple turned to him in surprise. His slight smile greeted her. "You are?"

"Yes." He touched the tip of her nose with his fingertip. "You're never boring. The night won't seem so long with you near me."

Temple stood still and watched the candlelight cast shadows on the strong planes of his face. Her heart hammered against her breast and she marveled at the depth of the emotions this man could call forth from her.

"Temple, once we're in the shelter, I don't want you to leave until I say you can. Understood?" He moved away from her and began gathering up the dirty dishes.

"Understood." Temple followed suit, and together they cleared the table. Her eyes found his, and her breath caught in her throat when she saw the expression there. Love? she wondered. Could it be?

"Good. I don't want anything to happen to you. I'd never forgive myself."

Temple watched as he walked from the room. She blew out the candles and stood for a moment in the dim room. Does he care for me? she mused. She squeezed her eyes shut and tried to stop hope from rising in her heart. After all, she told herself, she was here now, but later Candice would be back.

The whistle of the wind touched her ears, and she opened her eyes and saw the dark outline of the trees through the slits in the shutters. The tall shadows were swaying wildly, and the sight sent Temple running from the room to the man who, for her, meant strength and refuge from the rage of the oncoming hurricane.

Chapter Nine

When Temple woke up she narrowed her eyes against the surprisingly bright glow of the lamp. She let her lashes filter the light until her eyes became accustomed to the brightness.

The silence in the room sent an alarm through her, and she bolted upright. The empty shelter faced her.

"Zachary?" She looked wildly around the room. His pallet was empty. She scrambled to her feet, moving quickly toward the solid door at the bottom of the stairs. Zachary's warning sounded in her ears. No, I can't go out there, she thought. She glanced at her wristwatch. Three o'clock. The hurricane!

Temple's breath rasped in her throat. Had he gone outside and been trapped? Or . . . ? The thoughts gave birth to the terrifying image of Zachary trapped under a fallen tree, and Temple shut her eyes but couldn't shut out the horrible vision.

A rattle brought her eyes open again, and she held her breath and watched the door handle turn. She released her breath in a sigh of relief when she saw Zack walk confidently into the room.

"Oh, Zack!" Temple put a hand to her breast to still the frantic beat of her heart. "You scared the life out of me!"

He shook raindrops from his clothes. "Oh? Did you think I was the monster from the black lagoon?"

"No. I—I thought you might have gone outside and been hurt or . . . killed."

He ran his hand through his wet hair, and glistening drops of water fell to his broad shoulders. "And were you preparing to hustle out there and save me?"

Temple gazed at her clasped hands. "Well . . . I—I thought about it, but you told me to stay—"

"Exactly," he cut in. "I don't want you to venture out there—especially right now. I was just checking on the house."

"The house?" Temple's eyes widened as a mental vision of the house in ruins flitted through her mind. "It isn't . . . ?"

"Destroyed?" His mouth curved in a wry smile. "No, not yet. And if we're lucky, it won't be. Saint's Summit has survived hurricanes before."

Temple watched as he stripped the soaked raincoat from his muscular frame. "Has it hit yet?"

"No, but I expect it will within the hour." He wrapped a blanket around himself and eased down to sit on the floor. His fingers fumbled in the pocket of his discarded raincoat, and Temple stared at the silver flask he withdrew.

"What's that?"

"Whiskey. Want some?" He offered the flask to her.

Temple wrinkled her nose and shook her head. She watched his nonchalant shrug as he uncapped the container and took a long drink from the flask. A shiver coursed through his body, and he let his breath escape in an appreciative sigh. His dark eyes locked with hers for a moment; then he shook his head.

"And you can stop staring at me now. I'm chilled to the bone, and this is the best remedy, so you can save your scowls for someone else."

Temple flinched at his caustic tone. "I'm sorry, Zack. I didn't mean to judge you."

He sighed and leaned his head against the wall. His eyelids dropped to extinguish the dark glitter of his pupils. "Maybe I'm being too sensitive."

He sounded exhausted, and Temple's heart filled with love for him. She examined the deep lines etched at the corners of his mouth and along his forehead and read the fatigue and worry there.

"Will this night ever be over?"

At her whispered words his lids lifted and his dusky gaze met hers. One corner of his mouth lifted in a halfhearted smile.

"Come on," he told her, holding out a hand. "Let's go to sleep. By the time we wake up, it will all be over."

Temple looked at the large hand extended toward her and, almost against her will, she placed her own in his. Strong fingers gripped her hand, pulling her down to the floor. She sighed and nestled against his side. He wrapped his arms around her and pressed her head to his chest. Temple listened to the muffled beat of his heart and she felt the slight shiver of his body.

"You are cold, aren't you?"

He chuckled softly. "Frozen is a better word."

Temple snuggled closer and hugged him to her. "I'll warm you. Is that better?"

He was silent for a moment; then his voice reached her and his breath stirred a few strands of her hair. "So much better that I wonder if I can stand it."

Temple's breath stopped for a moment when she heard the accelerated beat of his heart. Her mind called out a warning, but it was accompanied by a thrill of excitement. She felt heady with the knowledge that she could arouse this man. She smiled and again tuned her ear to the beat of his heart. It was slower now; his breathing was regular. She closed her eyes and noticed that his shivering had stopped. Slowly she lifted her head to see if he was sleeping.

The ebony eyes sparkled in the dim light. She could just make out his lazy smile before it blurred and his lips took hers. The pressure of his mouth forced away the last of her sanity, and Temple answered his kiss with one of her own. Her lips moved against his, and she held her breath as the tip of his tongue traced her lips. She spread her fingers along his chest and felt the pounding of his heart.

He lifted his head and their gazes locked. "Ah,

my bewitching bride, how I love to pretend that you're truly mine."

His hand pressed her head to his chest again and kept it there. Temple felt the sting of tears in the corners of her eyes as the sadness of his words pierced her heart. She closed her eyes and tried to find the courage to risk everything and tell him that she loved him, but courage eluded her.

The dream was so real that Temple could feel the hard frame of Zachary's body. She could feel the tingle of his warm breath on her cheek and she could hear the air entering and leaving his lungs. Her nostrils twitched as she smelled the clean maleness of him, and a slow smile played on her lips.

Consciousness touched her, and she opened her eyes to stare at her spartan surroundings. She felt the rough blanket beneath her cheek and for a few moments wondered what had been real and what had been a dream. Her gaze wandered, finally fixing on the long legs that stretched beside her own. Zachary. She raised her head and examined his sleeping form. His chest rose and fell beneath her fingertips. His expression was vulnerable, his mouth soft and younger in sleep.

Temple resisted the urge to kiss his lips. She eased herself away from him and stood. She was stiff and she stretched protesting muscles. She eyed the door and wondered what lay beyond it. What time was it? she wondered.

She glanced at her watch. Eight o'clock!

Surely the hurricane had passed over the island by now. She started to wake Zachary, then paused. He looked exhausted, and she decided to let him sleep.

Quietly she crossed the small room to the door and slid back the bolt, then ran upstairs to confront the stone slab. Putting her shoulder to it, she pushed until it gave way. A bar of sunlight touched her face, and she smiled.

A burst of renewed energy shot through her, and she scrambled out of the dank shelter and into the sparkling sunlight. She stood rooted to the spot as her gaze took in the debris around her.

An uprooted tree lay before her, its gnarled roots twisted, with bits of earth still clinging to them. Gingerly she stepped around the tree and ran an eye over the house. The roof was damaged and shingles lay scattered along the lawn. A few of the shutters had been ripped from the house and several windowpanes had been shattered. Other than that, though, it seemed to have survived the storm intact.

Temple walked to the front of the house and grimaced when she saw the shrubs and flowering bushes that had been torn from the ground. Then she gasped when she took in the shards of glass that lay where the summerhouse had stood.

"Oh, no!" Temple stepped around the large, jagged pieces of glass and tried to remember how lovely the structure had been. She quickly moved away from the scattered shards and walked toward the edge of the cliff. The sea was choppy, and huge, white-crested waves lifted and crashed against the cliff walls.

The waters seemed to grow choppier and more violent as she watched. They leaped higher and higher, casting a spray of water over her. Droplets stung her face and arms, and she shivered. Foreboding swept over her, and she lifted her gaze to the sky. A swirling gray blanket met her gaze, and she backed away from the edge of the cliff.

Confusion filled her as she looked to her left, then right. Where was the sunshine? she wondered. It had been there a moment ago. A strong wind pushed her back, and she steadied herself with an effort. She felt her body sway as another gust of wind hit her. The debris at her feet began to stir in the swift wind, and suddenly Temple was frightened.

The sky looked angry now and the wind seemed to roar in her ears. Without warning, a sheet of rain fell from the black sky. Temple was soaked in seconds, and she looked around her in bewilderment. Everything was moving now. The debris formed small whirlpools around her knees, and the trees still left standing thrashed their limbs angrily.

"Temple!"

She stifled a scream as firm fingers spun her around to face the glowing embers in Zachary's eyes. She saw the firm line of his mouth and sensed his tightly checked anger.

"What do you think you're doing?" The words were delivered through clenched teeth.

"I—I thought—"

"You thought!" His upper lip curled in a sneer. "Come on! *Fast!*"

She grimaced as his fingers bit deeper into the soft flesh of her upper arm. He jerked her and she stumbled after him. A powerful gust of wind pushed her into him, and in that instant she felt him flinch, saw his arm shielding his face from some invisible threat. Temple blinked, then saw the blood that stained his shirt sleeve and colored his forehead. Before she had a chance to speak, he broke into a run. The violence of the storm seemed to build with each passing second, and Temple struggled to keep her fear at bay. She caught a glimpse of Zachary swiping at his forehead with his sleeve and she started to say something, but a ripping sound froze the words that formed on her tongue. She turned her head to see a tree branch crack and fall mere inches away from her.

Fear consumed her, and she felt tears scald her cheeks. She gasped as she felt herself being lifted from the ground and closed her eyes. Then there was a thump, and the crashing sounds diminished. Temple squeezed her eyes more tightly shut and wondered if she had slipped into unconsciousness.

It was then that she felt the warmth of Zachary's body as it shifted against hers. Her feet touched ground again, and she opened her eyes to find that they were inside the shelter once again. Safe, she thought. Safe and secure. She turned to Zack to thank him, then backed away from the fury she saw in his face. His black eyes bore into her and seemed to burn her wherever they touched.

"You damn near got us both killed!" His voice flayed her. "Do you have a death wish?"

"I—I thought it was over! The sun was shining!" Temple knew her faltering excuses sounded foolish. Besides, she *had* promised him that she wouldn't go out until he told her it was safe.

"The sun was shining," he mocked her. "It was the eye of the hurricane, you little idiot!" A trickle of blood from the wound on his forehead touched his left eye and he blinked.

Temple took a few steps toward him, wanting to wipe away the blood and cleanse the wound that she had caused. As if reading her mind, Zachary pushed past her and moved to the shelves.

"Leave me alone! You've caused enough trouble. I should have insisted that you join Mary and William," he muttered as he swept canned goods aside in search of a first-aid kit.

Uncontrollable rage stormed through Temple as she glared at his back. "I can't stand this anymore! I am *not* your slave! Just because you want me to do something, that doesn't mean I'm going to do it! And about the hurricane—so I made a mistake! Don't you ever make mistakes? Or are you too perfect to do something human once in a while?"

He turned slowly to face her, and his eyes glistened menacingly. "If you *would* obey me once in a while, you'd stay out of trouble."

Refusing to be stared down, Temple stood stiffly before him and kept her eyes locked with his. "The first time I listened to you, I married you, and it's been nothing but misery. I don't know how Giselle could stand it! I'm sick of playing second fiddle to the likes of Candice!"

He kept his eyes focused on her, but a shadow seemed to pass through them as he narrowed his gaze. "I don't much care for the feeling, either— and that's why I was in the process of divorcing Giselle at the time of her death."

His voice was low, but it carried easily and sent a tremor through Temple. The soft-spoken words penetrated her thoughts, and she stared at him, speechless, while he found the first-aid kit and moved to sit across from her.

He rested his back against the wall and opened the box. Once again he spoke to her, and his voice brimmed with sadness. "How little you know of me, Temple. Whose fault is that, I wonder? Mine? Or yours?"

Temple let her body go limp and slid to the floor. Her heart twisted painfully, and she stared at the carpet, unable to meet his eyes. If only she had known this before, she might have approached her marriage with a different attitude, and she might have been a happy woman today.

She heard the rustle of paper and lifted her gaze to Zack. He was fumbling with the first-aid kit.

"Can I help?"

He didn't look at her when he answered, "Yes. Be quiet and leave me alone."

The pain of his rejection shot through her, and she struggled to keep her tears from flowing. She watched as he cleaned the wound on his head, then turned his back on her and stretched out on the floor. She waited, then realized that he was going to sleep.

"Zack, you shouldn't sleep! If you have a concussion, you'll—"

"Spare me your concern," he interrupted. "I'm not sleeping."

Temple hugged her knees to her and rested her chin on them. She looked at her husband's back for a few minutes, then asked, "Zachary, why did Laura and Candice insinuate that you'd had affairs while you were married to Giselle, and that you'd made her miserable?"

For a moment she thought he wasn't going to answer her; then his voice reached her.

"Probably to get under your skin; and they succeeded, didn't they?" He shifted uncomfortably. "Laura was fond of Giselle, and she only knew what Giselle told her, which was mostly lies. Candice? She's always wanted to be a St. James."

"B-but Candice told me that she wasn't interested in marriage. That—that she liked her present arrangement."

Zack chuckled bitterly. "And you believed that?"

Temple felt her face flush. "Yes—in a way."

He laughed again. "Temple, Candice has proposed to *me* at least half a dozen times! You should have seen through her."

Temple nodded and felt like a total fool. Still, something nagged at her. "Zachary, you said you were divorcing Giselle. Why?"

His voice sounded weary, as if he'd gone over this a hundred times before. "I didn't see any need to continue the farce. She'd just wanted my money all along, and she'd already taken a lover."

"A lover!" Temple held her breath.

"Yes, the captain of one of my ships. I had already contacted a lawyer about the divorce when Giselle was killed in a plane crash. Her lover was with her; they were bound for Mexico."

"I see." Temple shook her head. "Why didn't you tell me this before?"

"Because what happened between Giselle and me is none of your concern. She has nothing to do with us."

"Hasn't she?" Temple frowned at his back. "Ever since I got here Laura's been comparing me with her."

She watched his shoulders shake as he laughed. "Comparing *you* to Giselle? If you were *anything* like Giselle I would never have married you. I learn from my mistakes. Or, at least, I thought I did."

Temple hesitated a moment. "But you loved her."

"I was infatuated with her."

"And what about Candice? Did you tell her about our . . . arrangement?"

He sighed deeply. "Of course not. I haven't

told anyone because it's nobody's business but ours."

Temple bit her lip to keep it from trembling. Candice hadn't known anything, after all; she had just been taking a shot in the dark. "Do you love her?"

He sighed again. "If I did, I would have married her long ago. She's nothing to me except a friend, and not a very close friend at that. She can be amusing, but she's hardly wife material."

And what about me? Temple wanted to ask, but she was afraid of what his answer would be. Instead, she let her gaze wander over his frame and wondered why Giselle would have taken a lover when she had Zachary St. James as a husband.

Chapter Ten

Temple listened to the constant tapping and wondered when the workers would be through repairing the roof. She ran a brush through her hair and tried to block out the noise.

"Temple!"

The sound made her jump, and she stared at the closed door of her bedroom. She blinked and shook her head when she realized that several of those taps she had been hearing had been made by Zack's knuckles on her door.

"Yes! Come in."

Instinctively she cringed when she saw the stormy expression on his face. What now? she wondered. She took a deep breath and waited.

"You have a visitor downstairs."

She frowned. "A visitor? Who?"

Zachary's mouth drew into a tight line. "Your old lover. I suppose he's come to take you back."

Temple's mind raced. Old lover? Who could it . . . ? She sucked in her breath and expelled it as she said, "Jeremy."

Zachary nodded. "Who else? Didn't you send for him?"

Temple stood and faced her husband. "Certainly not! If I had sent for him, I would have told you so. He's probably just concerned because he heard about the hurricane and wants to make sure that I'm all right."

The dark eyes mocked her. "Are you sure that's all he wants, my dear?"

Temple winced at the cruel way he used the endearment. "Yes, I'm sure."

"I see." Zachary opened the door. "Well, no matter what you think, he seems to have every intention of taking you back to the States." He gave her a terse smile. "Don't keep your guest waiting, Temple."

Temple watched the door close and balled her hands into tight fists. How cutting he could be, she thought.

She shrugged. She should be used to his attitude by now. Ever since the hurricane he had been cool and, at times, outright rude to her. How many times would she have to apologize for her hasty accusations? she wondered. At first, when he had told her the truth about Giselle and Candice, she had hoped that now things would be different between them. But in the weeks since the hurricane she had been forced to accept the futility of such a hope.

She shook her head and cast the worries from her mind. A blurred vision of Jeremy fixed itself in their place. Why was he here? she wondered. He couldn't have picked a worse time to show up on her doorstep. She certainly didn't need to give Zack another reason to be angry at her.

She straightened and made her way downstairs. When she entered the sitting room, Jeremy stood and offered her a wide smile.

"What a surprise, Jeremy! What brings you here?" Temple tried to return his smile but found it next to impossible. Her gaze swept the room and found it empty except for her uninvited guest.

"We were so worried about you, Temple! What with the hurricane and all . . ."

"Really? I've talked to Mom and Dad since the hurricane and assured them that I'm fine." Temple moved toward a chair and motioned for Jeremy to sit on the sofa.

Jeremy sat, then leaned toward her. "Yes, but I wasn't satisfied, so I took some of my vacation time and decided to come see for myself." His face mirrored his worry. "Are you happy?"

"Yes. Nothing at all is wrong, as you can see for yourself. I've been very busy, in fact. It's nice of you to concern yourself, but quite unnecessary. So tell me, how long will you be vacationing here?"

"A week." Jeremy seemed irritated at the change of topic and gave her a suspicious look. "I feel like you're not telling me something."

Temple bit back the sharp retort that first came to mind. Instead, she folded her hands in her lap and kept her tone quiet but firm. "Jeremy, things have changed. While I appreciate your concern, I do think you're meddling. I'm a married woman now and I'm not going to discuss my problems, if I have any, with you."

"So there are problems!" Jeremy smiled confidently.

"I didn't say that! I've been busy with my own life while Zack has his own job to do. Being Zachary's wife is very demanding—and very rewarding."

Jeremy's face tightened into a frown. He looked away from her, as if unable to face her confidence.

"It may seem to you that I married very hastily, Jeremy, but I want this marriage to work. You see—I love my husband." Jeremy looked startled, and Temple went on. "I love him very much."

Jeremy shook his head slowly. "I find that hard to believe."

"Well, it's the truth." Temple shrugged. "So if you've come to take me back to the States, I'm afraid you'll have to go home empty-handed."

Jeremy stared at her for a long moment. "You really mean that, don't you?"

Temple leaned forward and placed her hand over his. "I love Zachary with all my heart, Jeremy, and I never want to leave him." She pronounced each word carefully and with full confidence.

Jeremy sighed and closed his eyes for a moment. "Well, well. I must admit, I thought you'd be more than willing to come home with me next week. When I saw you last time I couldn't believe you would really go through with this marriage. And when you did, I was sure it wouldn't last."

"Zack is my husband, and this is my home."

"Yes." He glanced around the room. "I can see

179

that now." His gaze rested on Temple again. "I hope you'll be very happy."

"Thank you." She smiled and leaned back in her chair again. "So what will you be doing while you're on the island?"

"I thought I'd stay here for a day or two, soak up some sun, then go on to St. John." He grinned at her. "I can see how you fell in love with this place so quickly."

Temple laughed. "It's paradise, isn't it?" She thought for a moment, then made a decision and spoke before she had time to lose her nerve. "I've got a wonderful idea! Why not save tomorrow night so Zack and I can treat you to a night on the town?" *Who knows*, she thought to herself, *if it bothers Zack to see me with Jeremy maybe he'll take the time to pay a little attention to me himself.*

Jeremy moved uneasily on the sofa. "Well, I don't know . . ." He turned quickly at a slight sound, and his face paled.

Temple followed his gaze and saw that Zachary was entering the room with long, lazy strides. She swallowed and tried to control her growing nervousness. She was already regretting having made the offer, but it was too late to retract now. She would just have to face it out.

"Zack, you remember Jeremy, don't you?"

He turned his eyes briefly in her direction before letting his gaze settle on Jeremy. "Yes, I remember him. How are you?"

"Oh—oh, just great. I . . . uh . . . I'm here on vacation." Jeremy's forehead glistened with perspiration. "Well, I guess I'll be seeing you tomorrow night. Temple asked me . . ." His voice trailed off.

Temple's heart filled with love for Zack. Jeremy seemed like a frightened child in the face of Zack's cool control. Now, studying Jeremy's pale, boyish features, she wondered how she could ever have found him attractive.

Of course, she reminded herself, Jeremy had never managed to stir the embers of passion in her as Zachary had succeeded in doing. She studied her husband again and felt rivers of fire race through her veins. How easily he managed to affect her!

Suddenly Jeremy stood, as if no longer able to endure Zachary's penetrating stare. "Well, I—I'll be going back to my hotel now. Nice to see you both again."

Temple rose from her chair and planted a quick kiss on Jeremy's cheek. She felt him stiffen with apprehension. She glanced at Zachary and saw a cloud of anger darken his features before he pivoted sharply and left the room.

Jeremy breathed a sigh. "He's an explosive fellow, isn't he?"

"Yes." Temple tucked her hand in the crook of Jeremy's arm and walked with him to the front door. At the door she paused and looked up into his face. "We were always meant to be friends, Jeremy, never lovers."

He smiled. "Perhaps you're right."

"You'll phone and let us know for sure about tomorrow night?"

Jeremy shrugged. "Yes." He kissed her forehead. "I'll call you tomorrow in any case and we'll finalize our plans."

Temple nodded and watched him climb into his rented car and drive out of sight.

Well, I've done it now, she thought. I've severed the last tie to my former life.

She closed the door and turned back into the house. Her eyes widened and she gasped when she saw Zachary standing a few feet from her. A wicked smile curved his mouth and he nodded, as if confirming some inner knowledge, then turned and walked down the hall, out of her line of vision.

Temple shook her head to clear it. What was that all about? she wondered. The memory of his expression alarmed her. Is he going to ask me to leave? she wondered.

Her gaze roamed over the room. This *is* my home, she thought. But does Zachary want me here?

Temple stared at the golden wine in her goblet. Silence surrounded her, and she wondered if Zachary's parents had sensed her need to be alone with their son. Was that why they had retired to their room so early? They must have noticed how Zachary had avoided her in the days since they had returned home from their cruise.

Temple cleared her throat and shifted her gaze from the wine goblet to the man who stood and stared out the window into the black night.

"Your parents seemed to have enjoyed the cruise, Zack."

"Hmmm."

Temple frowned and decided on a change of subject. "Are you going to rebuild *Saint's Escape*, or was it too badly damaged in the hurricane?"

"It's beyond repair."

"So you'll build a new one?"

"I don't see much point in it."

Temple's frown deepened. "But I thought you loved the yacht!"

Now he turned slowly to face her. "I've changed my mind about a lot of things lately. Love . . . That's a fickle feeling. Don't you agree?"

His words seemed to twist like a knife in her heart, and Temple took a long drink of her wine in an effort to avoid his penetrating gaze.

"So you have no opinion?" he pressed her.

Temple sighed and placed her goblet on the table. "I don't agree with you, if that's what you're asking."

"And you're such an expert, of course."

"You asked for my opinion and you got it!" Temple met his steady gaze. "Why don't we clear the air on the *real* issues that are bothering us?"

Zachary bowed slightly. "After you."

Temple plucked at the soft green fabric of her gown and felt her nerve ends fray. "Very well. I'd like to know why you're being so . . . aloof."

Zachary shoved his hands into the pockets of

his dark trousers. "I'm keeping my distance to see what develops."

"Develops?" Temple rose from the chair. "What do you mean? What do you *think* is going to develop?"

He shrugged. "I'm not sure what's going on around here anymore. First you had me marked as an unfaithful husband, and then your old boyfriend shows up and tells me he's come for you. Is it your turn to be unfaithful now?"

Temple winced at his cutting words. "I told Jeremy I wasn't going back with him." She took a step toward Zachary but paused when she saw a strange gleam come into his eyes. "I didn't send for him. And I've apologized a hundred times for jumping to conclusions about you." She smiled ruefully as she went on. "I know you're disappointed about the way things have gone for us, and I don't blame you for being angry with me. I take full responsibility for this mess we call a marriage."

An exasperated sigh reached her ears, and she turned to face him again. Zachary ran a hand through his hair and stared at the carpet.

"I can't let you do that, Temple. I'm partly to blame. I should never have blackmailed you into marriage. It's just that I thought—"

"It wasn't blackmail; I knew what I was doing," Temple interrupted him. She hated to see the hurt that had settled on his face. Deep lines were etched along the sides of his mouth, and Temple wanted only to erase those lines with her fingertips. "*I* used *you*."

A bitter smile found his lips. "Used me?" He

shook his head and chuckled without mirth. "I don't think so." He held up a protesting hand when she started to speak. "No. Listen to me. You're free to leave. I won't hold you to our bargain any longer. You're young and you deserve to be happy. I was being selfish and I have no right to insist that you cater to my fantasies."

"Fantasies?" Temple echoed, but her mind whirled as she tried to digest his words. Was he really ending their marriage? she wondered. Tears blurred her vision. Was it really all over? Didn't he want her, even for a year?

"Yes, fantasies." Again he laughed mirthlessly. "I thought I could make you love me. I thought—I made myself believe—that after a few months of living with me you'd fall in love with me. But things like that just can't be arranged. I should have known that."

"You're telling me to leave? That you . . . that you love me but you want me to leave?" She hardly dared speak the words, sure that he would read the hope in her voice.

Zachary threw her a puzzled look. "I'm giving you your freedom, yes. I know you've been unhappy here."

"Only because I felt—I felt that . . ." Temple swallowed, unable to find the words to express her feelings.

Zachary watched her for a moment, then took a hesitant step in her direction. "Because you felt *what*, Temple?"

"I was confused! I thought at first I knew you, but then I heard those things and I—I—was so mixed up!" She wiped the tears from her eyes.

"Who are you, Zachary? Are you the man I met in the hotel that day? I feel as if I don't know you at all."

"Where you're concerned, I thought I was an open book." He tilted his head to one side. "Perhaps I was wrong."

In two long strides he was in front of her, and his breath stirred her hair. Strong fingers found her upper arms and he pulled her to him, forcing her to throw her head back so that she could look at him.

"Little fool! Don't you *know* that I'm in love with you?"

Temple felt her throat constrict with sudden emotion. She shook her head in mute answer.

Dark eyebrows met over ebony eyes. "I am. But it's caused me nothing but agony, Temple, and only you can stop my pain by giving your love to me in return. Do I have it?"

Temple sighed and wrapped her arms around his neck. Her fingers found the curls at his nape and she pulled his head down so that their lips could meet. All the doubts she had harbored about this man seemed to slip away as his lips moved against hers. Her lips parted, and he deepened the kiss while one hand slipped to cover her firm breast.

When he finally untangled himself from her embrace, Temple felt as if part of her soul had been ripped from her. "Don't leave me, Zachary. I couldn't bear that."

Relief made her weak when she saw the passion sparkle in the depths of his eyes.

"I won't leave you, Temple; I just want to get a few things straight before I lose control completely." He smiled and stepped back, putting more distance between them. "First, you must know that what I feel for you is much deeper, much stronger, than what I felt for Giselle. We're all entitled to a few mistakes, and I made them all with her. She wanted a rich husband, and I obliged." He shrugged, and pain flitted over his face. "I was a fool and I discovered it too late. The whole thing left me feeling . . . alone . . . and I turned to Candice." His dark brows met. "But I never loved Candice, and when I met you I quickly forgot her. You must believe that!"

Temple swallowed the emotion in her throat. "I do."

His smile returned. "When I met you, everyone seemed to pale in comparison. How I wanted you! I felt that I couldn't let you leave my life, so I roped you into this crazy marriage."

"I'm so glad." Temple ached to hold him.

Relief flooded his expression, and he uttered a sigh of relief. "Temple, I must tell you that I married you because I love you. I'll always love you, songbird. I want nothing more than to have you with me until the end of my time on earth."

A sob tore through Temple's throat, and she stumbled into his embrace. Longing filled her, and she slipped her hands inside Zachary's dinner jacket and caressed his chest through his soft silk shirt. "I love you, body and soul." She kissed his shirtfront and then moved her hands to slip the jacket from his shoulders. As she began unbuttoning his shirt, her eyes met his. "We've wasted too much time, Mr. St. James."

He laughed, and this time it was genuine. His lips touched her shoulder and his hands caressed her bare back. "What fun we'll have catching up on that lost time, Mrs. St. James."

Temple sighed. "I wish we still had the yacht and we could board her and be alone for weeks and weeks."

Zachary touched her lips with his. "We'll have another one, then, if that's what you want. But what do we need a yacht for when I own a cruise line?"

"We'll go on a cruise?" Temple questioned.

"Yes. How would you like to take a honeymoon cruise?" He smiled. "We'll pretend it's a slow boat to China."

Temple giggled. "What a wonderful idea! I met you because I was upset at not being allowed on a ship, and now I'm going to board her with the owner himself—for our honeymoon!"

"A honeymoon does sound better than a mere job, doesn't it?"

"Definitely."

Zachary bent his head and kissed her, and Temple surrendered herself to her husband and to the passion that only he could evoke.

IT'S YOUR OWN SPECIAL TIME

Contemporary romances for today's women.

Each month, six very special love stories will be yours

from SILHOUETTE.

Look for them wherever books are sold

or order now from the coupon below.

$1.50 each

__# 1 PAYMENT IN FULL Hampson	__#28 MAN OF THE OUTBACK Hampson
__# 2 SHADOW AND SUN Carroll	__#29 RAIN LADY Wildman
__# 3 AFFAIRS OF THE HEART Powers	__#30 RETURN ENGAGEMENT Dixon
__# 4 STORMY MASQUERADE Hampson	__#31 TEMPORARY BRIDE Halldorson
__# 5 PATH OF DESIRE Goforth	__#32 GOLDEN LASSO Michaels
__# 6 GOLDEN TIDE Stanford	__#33 A DIFFERENT DREAM Vitek
__# 7 MIDSUMMER BRIDE Lewis	__#34 THE SPANISH HOUSE John
__# 8 CAPTIVE HEART Beckman	__#35 STORM'S END Stanford
__# 9 WHERE MOUNTAINS WAIT Wilson	__#36 BRIDAL TRAP McKay
__#10 BRIDGE OF LOVE Caine	__#37 THE BEACHCOMBER Beckman
__#11 AWAKEN THE HEART Vernon	__#38 TUMBLED WALL Browning
__#12 UNREASONABLE SUMMER Browning	__#39 PARADISE ISLAND Sinclair
__#13 PLAYING FOR KEEPS Hastings	__#40 WHERE EAGLES NEST Hampson
__#14 RED, RED ROSE Oliver	__#41 THE SANDS OF TIME Owen
__#15 SEA GYPSY Michaels	__#42 DESIGN FOR LOVE Powers
__#16 SECOND TOMORROW Hampson	__#43 SURRENDER IN PARADISE Robb
__#17 TORMENTING FLAME John	__#44 DESERT FIRE Hastings
__#18 THE LION'S SHADOW Hunter	__#45 TOO SWIFT THE MORNING Carroll
__#19 THE HEART NEVER FORGETS Thornton	__#46 NO TRESPASSING Stanford
__#20 ISLAND DESTINY Fulford	__#47 SHOWERS OF SUNLIGHT Vitek
__#21 SPRING FIRES Richards	__#48 A RACE FOR LOVE Wildman
__#22 MEXICAN NIGHTS Stephens	__#49 DANCER IN THE SHADOWS Wisdom
__#23 BEWITCHING GRACE Edwards	__#50 DUSKY ROSE Scott
__#24 SUMMER STORM Healy	__#51 BRIDE OF THE SUN Hunter
__#25 SHADOW OF LOVE Stanford	__#52 MAN WITHOUT A HEART Hampson
__#26 INNOCENT FIRE Hastings	__#53 CHANCE TOMORROW Browning
__#27 THE DAWN STEALS SOFTLY Hampson	__#54 LOUISIANA LADY Beckman

Silhouette Romance

___#55 WINTER'S HEART Ladame
___#56 RISING STAR Trent
___#57 TO TRUST TOMORROW John
___#58 LONG WINTER'S NIGHT Stanford
___#59 KISSED BY MOONLIGHT Vernon
___#60 GREEN PARADISE Hill
___#61 WHISPER MY NAME Michaels
___#62 STAND-IN BRIDE Halston
___#63 SNOWFLAKES IN THE SUN Brent
___#64 SHADOW OF APOLLO Hampson
___#65 A TOUCH OF MAGIC Hunter
___#66 PROMISES FROM THE PAST Vitek
___#67 ISLAND CONQUEST Hastings
___#68 THE MARRIAGE BARGAIN Scott
___#69 WEST OF THE MOON St. George
___#70 MADE FOR EACH OTHER Afton Bonds
___#71 A SECOND CHANCE ON LOVE Ripy
___#72 ANGRY LOVER Beckman
___#73 WREN OF PARADISE Browning
___#74 WINTER DREAMS Trent
___#75 DIVIDE THE WIND Carroll
___#76 BURNING MEMORIES Hardy

___#77 SECRET MARRIAGE Cork
___#78 DOUBLE OR NOTHING Oliver
___#79 TO START AGAIN Halldorson
___#80 WONDER AND WILD DESIRE Stephens
___#81 IRISH THOROUGHBRED Roberts
___#82 THE HOSTAGE BRIDE Dailey
___#83 LOVE LEGACY Halston
___#84 VEIL OF GOLD Vitek
___#85 OUTBACK SUMMER John
___#86 THE MOTH AND THE FLAME Adams
___#87 BEYOND TOMORROW Michaels
___#88 AND THEN CAME DAWN Stanford
___#89 A PASSIONATE BUSINESS James
___#90 WILD LADY Major
___#91 WRITTEN IN THE STARS Hunter
___#92 DESERT DEVIL McKay
___#93 EAST OF TODAY Browning
___#94 ENCHANTMENT Hampson
___#95 FOURTEEN KARAT BEAUTY Wisdom
___#96 LOVE'S TREACHEROUS JOURNEY Beckman
___#97 WANDERER'S DREAM Clay
___#98 MIDNIGHT WINE St. George
___#99 TO HAVE, TO HOLD Camp

SILHOUETTE BOOKS, Department SB/1
1230 Avenue of the Americas
New York, NY 10020

Please send me the books I have checked above. I am enclosing
$_____ (please add 50¢ to cover postage and handling. NYS and
NYC residents please add appropriate sales tax). Send check or
money order—no cash or C.O.D.'s please. Allow six weeks for delivery.

NAME_____

ADDRESS_____

CITY_____STATE/ZIP_____

Silhouette Romance

15-Day Free Trial Offer
6 Silhouette Romances

6 Silhouette Romances, free for 15 days! We'll send you 6 new Silhouette Romances to keep for 15 days, absolutely free! If you decide not to keep them, send them back to us. You pay nothing.

Free Home Delivery. But if you enjoy them as much as we think you will, keep them by paying us the retail price of just $1.50 each. We'll pay all shipping and handling charges. You'll then automatically become a member of the Silhouette Book Club, and will receive 6 more new Silhouette Romances every month and a bill for $9.00. That's the same price you'd pay in the store, but you get the convenience of home delivery.

Read every book we publish. The Silhouette Book Club is the way to make sure you'll be able to receive every new romance we publish.

READERS' COMMENTS ON
SILHOUETTE ROMANCES:

"Your books are written with so much feeling and quality that they make you feel as if you are part of the story."

—D.C.*, Piedmont, SC

"I'm very particular about the types of romances I read; yours more than fill my thirst for reading."

—C.D., Oxford, MI

"I hope Silhouette novels stay around for many years to come. . . . Keep up the good work."

—P.C., Frederick, MD

"What a relief to be able to escape in a well-written romantic story."

—E.N.. Santa Maria, CA

"Silhouette Romances . . . Fantastic!"

—M.D., Bell, CA

"I'm pleased to be adding your books to my collection—my library is growing in size every day."

—B.L., La Crescenta, CA

* Names available on request.